Words from a Glass Bubble

VANESSA GEBBIE is the daughter of a student nurse and a travelling salesman and was given up for adoption at birth. She spent much of her childhood in Wales and can still sing hymns and swear in Welsh. Her short fiction has won many awards including Fish and Bridport prizes and has been published in the UK, USA, New Zealand, Canada and India, translated into Vietnamese and Italian and broadcast by the BBC. Her teaching and facilitating has led to the publishing of anthologies of work by both the homeless and refugees in her home city of Brighton and Hove, Sussex, UK. Her novel in progress won a first prize in the 2007 *Daily Telegraph* Novel Competition.

VANESSA GEBBIE

WORDS *from*
A GLASS BUBBLE

SALT

CAMBRIDGE

PUBLISHED BY SALT PUBLISHING

14a High Street, Fulbourn, Cambridge CB21 5DH United Kingdom

First published 2008

Printed and bound in the United Kingdom by Lightning Source UK Ltd

Typeset in Swift 11 / 14

ISBN 978 1 84471 399 8 hardback
ISBN 978 1 84471 734 7 paperback

Salt Publishing Ltd gratefully acknowledges
the financial assistance of Arts Council England

13 5 7 9 8 6 4 2

In memory of a good friend, Jan Newton.

CONTENTS

Vanessa Gebbie

Words *from* a Glass Bubble

WORDS FROM A GLASS BUBBLE

THE VIRGIN MARY spoke to Eva Duffy from a glass bubble in a niche halfway up the stairs. Eva, the post woman, heard the Virgin's words in her stomach more than in her ears, and she called her the VM. The VM didn't seem to mind. She was plastic, six inches high, hand painted, and appeared to be growing out of a mass of very green foliage and very pink flowers, more suited to a fish tank. She held a naked Infant Jesus who stretched his arms out to Eva and mouthed, every so often, 'Carry?'

The VM's words were unfailingly meaningful, but often ungrammatical.

'It will be the porcelain and silver effigies that speak properly,' Eva said. And anyway, this VM had to speak out of the corner of her mouth where her pink lipstick had smudged.

She also appeared to have a wall eye. That would be the sloppy painting in the VM factory according to Connor, Eva's bricklayer husband, who never stopped on the stairs to find out if she spoke to him, too. 'No one's perfect,' Eva said.

Connor had a port wine stain on his left cheek in the shape of Cyprus with a few undiscovered islands under his ear. He had the habit of turning sideways when he spoke. He turned sideways on the stairs too, didn't look at the niche. Eva mumbled enough *Hail Marys* for the two of them every time she went up

1

or down; she always picked up a small oval photo frame from the shelf, said, 'How's Little Declan keeping?' and kissed it. More gilt than silver after twenty-four years of kissing.

That particular day, standing at the turn of the stairs, holding her only baby's photo, Eva heard a dog bark twice somewhere on the estate. That was a good sign. She replaced the photo with the VM's bubble to one side and, on the other, the phial of Holy Water from Lourdes brought by Mrs Flynn after Declan was taken with the asthma.

Also, instead of saying one thing for Eva to think about on her post round, the VM said two: '. . . but we live in cavernous times,' she said. That was the usual meaningful bit. At least, Eva supposed it was so. She patted Declan, made to go on down the stairs. But the VM spoke again in Eva's stomach. 'Don't you go delivering no letters to that Finn Piper,' she said.

'Why ever not?' Eva's mouth said. There was no reply from the VM. Eva's heart said, 'I can't be promising that. It's not up to me who gets their letters.' What was a post woman after all said and done but a carrier of people's questions and answers? It would not do to short-circuit the process.

Ah, but it may have been a safe thing to be promising what the VM wanted. In all those years of being post woman, there'd not been so much as a weekly cut-price promotion leaflet from the Stores to take up the four mile track to Finn Piper's farm. 'Mad as a box of frogs,' said those with opinions, and the kids from the estate cycled up there on fine evenings, threw stones at what was left of the windows to make Finn angry, and no one said not.

Finn Piper would rumble deep in his throat and screech like a night owl, throwing his voice round about the pine trees. He would *ack ack* like the blackest of the crows and *honk* like the oldest ravens in the crags. His black-bearded face would appear in first this window then that, as he flapped his hands and screeched, and the estate boys would set up a howling and a barking back. But none of them could make the sound of the birds like Finn Piper, and they never stayed up there when dusk fell to hear the thin cry of the buzzard rising from the old chimneys into the night sky.

But that was the day that Eva Duffy did have a letter to take to Finn Piper.

It was a Wednesday. The writing on the envelope was a child's, the stamp was askew, and it had been posted locally a week before. Must have got caught up. Eva kept that letter until last, and drove the van as far as she could up a muddy track, parking by a tubular metal gate, padlocked and tied to its post with blue string. There were gorse bushes on either side. Eva hoiked her skirt up and stood on the second bar of the gate, swung a leg over the top and dropped onto the mud. One foot slid into a brown puddle.

That was the VM reminding her not to give Finn Piper any letters. 'What do you know about being a post woman?' Eva muttered, rubbing her shoe with spit and a finger. She had two miles further to go, stepping round cowpats and sheep droppings, scattering knots of dirty-bummed ewes, before she reached Finn Piper's farm.

The front door was open. Chickens were scratching in the mud, both inside and outside the house. There was no letter box. Eva put her head round the door. It was very dark. No convenient hall table on which to place the post.

3

'Mr Piper?' Eva called, but the dampness ate her words.

She fetched a flat stone from the wall and put it on the ground just inside the door, placing the letter addressed to *Mister Finn Birdman* on the stone where he would not miss it. Then she shouted his real name once more before retracing her steps. But only a short way. It was the twittering of a flock of sparrows approaching that stopped her, and she ducked behind the stone wall, to hide rather than to spy.

But she did spy. The bearded figure of Finn Piper came loping and twittering across the meadow swinging an old green enamel saucepan, naked as the day he was delivered. Two collies followed, low to the ground. He crossed the yard to his house, and the twittering stopped as he put the saucepan down, slopping water onto the mud. He looked round, and Eva ducked again. She counted twenty. When she peered over the wall, he was sitting on a tree stump with his back to her, holding the letter, and as she watched he raised it to his face, sniffed at it, and carefully bit one corner as though he was testing for gold.

Later, Eva talked to the VM. 'It was the back of his neck,' she said.

'What was?'

'Ah. Like a little boy's. Vulnerable.'

'Needing a wash, more like.' The VM's mouth seemed a little pinched tonight. She hefted the Infant Jesus, who was out of proportion with his Mother—big enough for a three year old—higher on her arm. 'I were watching.'

'I thought so,' said Eva. 'I could feel something like your breath on my own neck.'

4

Eva, in bed, couldn't talk to Connor about little boy's necks. So she said, 'Took a letter to that Finn Piper today. Been in this job twenty years, give or take. First one.'

Connor chuckled into his pillow, facing the other way. 'Mad as a box of frogs.'

'They all say that.' Eva watched the streetlight striping the Artex through the curtain rings. She sighed. 'I wonder . . .'

'Wonder what, then?'

'If Finn Piper can read.'

Connor sat up and turned on the light. His hair was sticking up. Cyprus was looking redder, it always did that when he was tired. 'Now don't you go interfering . . .'

'I can't take you seriously with your hair like that,' she said. 'Put the light out and go to sleep.' 'And,' Eva could have said, 'you are beginning to sound like the VM.' But she didn't.

The next day Eva had no spare time, but on the Friday she took an extra bag in the post van. Connor's old painting trousers. A few jumpers, patched but fine. A new orange shirt that Connor hadn't liked, still in its cellophane. She'd carried the bag downstairs, holding it to her left side so the VM would miss it.

She didn't. 'Taking them someplace nice then?' she said.

'None of your business,' Eva's heart said, as her mouth said, 'The needy.' And she'd paused in the kitchen and added half a chocolate sponge wrapped in foil.

Finn Piper, barefoot but dressed this time in old jeans and a grey plastic raincoat, was tying a long length of blue twine round and round the trunk of a half-dead pine tree. He must have seen Eva sidestepping the chickens but he didn't look up or say a word.

5

'Mr Piper?' Eva said, staying twenty feet or so back.

'Ah.' Finn Piper curled the twine over and under itself into a complicated knot and let it hang like a tassel from the tree. He stood back.

'It's a tree alright,' he said.

'It is that.' Eva said. 'And very handsome it looks too.'

He smiled, made a noise deep in his throat, a soft rumble, the cooing of a pigeon.

'I wondered,' Eva said. And the VM's voice came from nowhere as always, 'I'd say you got thirty seconds to change your mind, love.'

Eva took a deep breath. 'I wondered,' she said firmly, 'if you'd read the letter from the other day, or whether . . .'

'Ah,' Finn Piper said, pulling the crumpled envelope from his mac pocket, handing it to her. It was torn. Through the tear she could see enough of the contents to know what it was.

There was a pause.

'Lucky thing,' Eva said.

'Lord love us,' said the VM. 'Will you leave it, Eva Duffy?'

Later, back home on the stairs, the VM didn't say anything. 'Go on,' Eva said, after a few breathless *Hail Marys*. 'Tell me you told me so.'

The VM didn't reply. Her wall eye seemed to be looking over Eva's shoulder, the plastic chin was more tilted than usual, the mouth even more pinched. But the Infant waved his arms and blew a spit-bubble.

In bed that night, Eva rubbed Connor's back.

'So how did it go?' he said.

'How did what go?'

'Get on with you, woman,' said Connor. 'You had chicken shit all over your work shoes.'

Eva sighed. 'He couldn't read,' she said.

'And?'

'He's never been to a kid's party, either.'

Connor didn't move. But Eva felt something unsteady creeping under the muscles of his back.

Later, hours later, Eva lay there, eyes closed. Connor was awake, she could feel it through the mattress. A tautness. Sleep would not come to her, held away by memories as insistent as a flock of starlings on new grass seed.

Nursery rhymes. Earnest adult voices over the plinking of a xylophone.

'Girls and boys come out to PLAY
The moon doth shine as bright as DAY . . . '

The smell of food. Sandwiches, crisps, little sausages, bright jellies in paper cups. Giggles. Kids laughing. Adults talking. The rattle and bell of some plastic toy. Declan coughing. Declan coughing. Declan . . .

'Wee Willie Winkie runs through the TOWN,
Upstairs and downstairs in his night GOWN . . .'

Every sound and smell a shard of pain. Eva couldn't focus on what Declan's face looked like. Every time she tries, she just sees balloons. Hears the xylophone, then a click. How still everything went, suddenly, and the wail of an ambulance cutting through the quiet.

Mothers sliding away with their toddlers.

Connor climbing down from a dirty white pick-up still wearing his hard hat, following the ambulance men in through the glass door.

7

'What?'

A half-eaten yellow jelly baby trodden into the hall carpet.

Eva, in bed, waited. Sleep came to Connor in the end, just before dawn, but not to Eva. She slipped out of bed and went half way down the stairs, didn't say anything with her mouth, but sat, head in hands, while her heart said things about memories rising up, about a squished jelly baby.

The VM sniffed. 'Well, can I say it now?' she said.

'Go on.'

'I told you not to take Finn Piper no letters. I said . . .'

'I know what you said.'

This was early Saturday, and Eva was working the morning shift. She got ready slower than usual, sat on the bed for a while and watched Connor snoring. The day seemed weighted down. And it was that day that the VM again said two things for Eva to think about.

'Life,' she said, 'ain't no bowl of cherries.' Eva ignored this one; it said nothing she didn't know anyway. She picked up Declan's photo, kissed it, and the VM said, 'You be enjoying yourselves, now.'

The VM wasn't looking at her any more. Her bad eye seemed to have slipped sideways and she was looking past Eva with the other eye, like there was something important on the wall behind her. Eva didn't answer with her heart or her mouth. She went to replace Declan in the niche, when something in what the VM had said came back at her like an echo and bounced around in her heart. 'You be enjoying yourselves . . .'

Eva picked up the VM's bubble and turned it over. The glass was sealed at the base with a black plastic plug. The VM's voice

8

was somewhat muffled, 'What in the name of Paddy O'Neill are you up to?' she said. 'I can't breathe upside-down.'

Eva pushed Declan's photo deep into her hip pocket.

It didn't take much effort with a kitchen knife to loosen the VM's plug. 'Will you be telling me what's going on?' said the VM, who, being attached to the plug with a dab of hard yellow glue, lay in Eva's hand, her fronds of green plastic foliage and bright pink flowers scattered over the lino. Her bubble lay on its side on the table, completely empty.

'This might hurt a bit, sorry,' said Eva's heart, as she slid the knife between the VM's robes (she didn't seem to have feet) and the base. The base fell away and rolled under the table.

'Ow,' said the VM.

'Wheee!' said The Infant, his face glowing.

'There.' Eva inserted them both into her breast pocket, from where the VM's face peered like a small boy's pet mouse in a blue hood.

'And me,' said The Infant, face against the inside of Eva's pocket.

'Sorry,' Eva said, folding a handkerchief and pushing it underneath the VM so that he could see out too. 'Now. I've got to get to work.'

All morning, the VM grumbled. 'Me, who's never travelled,' she said as Eva did her round on the estate. 'What's this?' she said, as Eva put her head round the door of the corner shop on Limerick Street and put their letters on the counter. 'Never been here, ugly place,' she said, as Eva sent a load of brochures and brown envelopes tumbling through the glass doors of the factory office.

'Be an angel and drop us off home?' the VM said at the end of the morning.

'I'm no angel,' Eva said.

'Please? I don't want to go near no kids' parties.'

'No,' Eva said.

It was windy at Finn Piper's farm just before two that after-noon. He was sitting on his tree stump, party invitation in one hand, the other on the neck of one of his collies. He had tied up the orange shirt—still in its cellophane packet—with blue twine, and had hung it from the pine tree, where it moved in the breeze, shining and twisting like an ill-conceived kite. He had put on Connor's painting trousers and his legs stuck out of the ends like sticks of celery. Connor's v-necked red jumper had something indefinable down the front.

The VM sniffed. 'If there's one thing I can't be doing with . . .'

'. . . it's snobbery,' Eva finished the sentence as she picked her way across the yard. Finn beamed up at her, opened his mouth wide and crowed, a long doodle-doo that sent a flight of rooks skyward. The chickens grubbing about his bare feet looked up for a second, then resumed their work.

All the way down the track, all the way along the road into town, Finn Piper sat hunched in the passenger seat of the post van, his arms round his knees, craning his neck to see what was passing, then nodding to himself. The van smelled of earth and river water. Occasionally, the shrieks of eagles split the air, nearly sending Eva off the road.

'Will you be taking more care, Eva Duffy?' said her pocket.

Finn called out the names of things as they passed. 'It's the sheep alright. It's a field alright. It's horses alright. It'll be men alright. It's a house. A house.'

It was a house, but it was a poor one. The front gate swung on one hinge, and there were a few toys strewn to one side of a stained and cracked concrete path. A rusty tricycle, a ball, a plastic bucket and spade. A half-empty sand pit. A larger child's bicycle with a flat tyre lay on the grass in front of a football goal made from bean sticks and string. Hanging from the letter box was a single green balloon.

The presence of the post woman here on a Saturday afternoon was odd enough, but the sight of Finn Piper on the estate had roused a small gaggle of boys who watched Eva knock on the door. She heard the yap of a dog from inside the house, then another and another behind them on the road. She turned and two lads laughed, then fell quiet.

A small boy in a red jersey opened the door, a toddler clutching his leg.

'Mam!' The bigger boy shouted back into the house. 'He's here. It's Mister Finn Birdman.' Then, to Finn Piper, he said, 'I wrote it, by myself, nearly. I didn't think you'd come. It's not my birthday, it's his.' He nodded at his leg, looking faintly embarrassed. 'Can you show us how to make your bird noises? Please?'

Finn Piper just stood, head on one side.

The toddler's nose needed wiping. Eva Duffy patted Finn Piper on the back. 'Go on,' she said. 'I'll be back at five thirty. Enjoy yourself.'

An older boy appeared from the shadows, another toddler on his hip. Finn Piper growled, an old pigeon. He didn't move. The middle lad looked back into the house, and Eva could hear it now—the plink of a xylophone, earnest adults singing nursery rhymes, children giggling, the rattle and bell of a plastic toy.

11

'Go on with you,' the older boy said to Finn, 'They'll not eat you.' He turned to Eva, his eyes flicking to her pocket. 'Would you come in too?' he asked.

Eva felt Finn Piper slide his hand into hers. She felt her other hand deep in her hip pocket, her fingers finding and curling tight round a small oval frame. She felt an intake of breath from the VM. Then Eva, whose head did not want to go in at all, stepped over the threshold.

～

It was late, late in the evening when Connor helped Eva put the VM back in her bubble. The VM seemed to be smiling, although her eyes were puffy, and that was maybe tiredness. The Infant's cheeks shone, but then the light in the kitchen was bright.

Connor glued the VM back to her base, reassembled the foliage, and put her bubble back together with the help of some masking tape.

'Good as new,' he said.

Eva sat at the kitchen table, hands round a cup of tea. 'You should have been there,' she said. 'Like the bird house at the zoo, it was, in the end. Listen—' and she cuckooed, but softly, so as not to disturb the neighbours.

Connor said nothing, but picked up the VM's bubble and Declan's photo and took them up to the niche. He was a long time coming down.

Later, when Eva started snoring, Connor got out of bed, fetched Declan out of the niche, and sat on the stairs in his pyjamas. He held the photo gently, turning it this way then that, letting the lights from the estate pick out his son's curls, his nose, his birthmark. Declan's own little island; more like Malta than Cyprus.

Cyprus felt hot tonight, but it didn't seem to matter. Connor didn't turn his head away, but looked straight at the VM.

'Hello?' he said, then listened. And he might just have heard a reply, somewhere inside him, somewhere near his stomach perhaps, or his heart,

'You'll be Declan's Dad then? About time.'

Later, in bed, Eva patted his back.

'You're awake?' he said.

'I am,' said Eva. 'Where've you been?'

'Nowhere,' Connor said. 'Go to sleep, will you?' Then he said, 'I've got one question. Why did you take the statue with you?'

'Just for company,' Eva said with her mouth. 'I took her along for company.' But her heart said, 'We were holding each other's hands.'

Then, there was a sound. The cry of a buzzard as it might have been made by a small boy, a thin little cry that rose triumphant into the post woman's house, echoed round the stairs and floated out of the open windows to disappear among the whispers of wind in the night sky.

13

'I CAN SQUASH THE KING, TOMMO'

WHEN THE WIND is in the east, coming just steady over the coal tips, the tunnel on the old Merthyr coal line sings like an empty pop bottle. The sound bells about the soot and bricks as if it's caught in the throat of a Dowlais tenor, coaldust and all, then it spills out and flows down the valley to the town. It settles between the council houses, seeps through the gaps in the windows; a *hooooooo*ing that has children crying there's ghosts in the chimney. Then Ianto 'Passchendaele' Jenkins, in khaki, stops his begging on the steps of the cinema and lifts a finger into the air, like he's conducting.

If the wind is stronger, it sets the big old iron rocking horse going on its tarmac square behind the High Street, and it squeaks, squeaks, squeaks like there's a football team of little lads astride, some standing. The swings on their brown chains swing with no hands to push. Back, forth. Squeak, squeak And sheets of newspaper blow across the tarmac, swirling with bus tickets and sweet wrappers in a demented ballet, piling against the doors of Ebenezer Chapel to make work for the Minister.

Passchendaele Jenkins lifts his finger into the air and looks up at the windows of the Savings Bank, watching for Tommo Price to move. And Batty Annie, her hair like string, leaves the door of the old linesman's hut swinging on its one hinge, and stumbles, bent, along the tracks in her slippers waving a shrimping net that's full of nothing but holes. She's fetching her son home.

Wait for me, Lovely Boy . . .

Then Tommo Price, wearing a suit, looks out of his window at the Savings Bank, watches Batty Annie bent into the wind disappearing behind the council houses on her way to the tunnel. He will shake his head before going back to his ledgers. And the figures on the paper will be blown about as he watches. And Tommo will push his chair back, call across to Mr Billy Harris, Deputy Manager, that he has to go out. Billy Harris will nod and carry on pulling a thread from his sleeve as he talks to the publican's wife on the telephone.

By the time Tommo gets to the tunnel, Annie will be inside, her slippers soft on the moss and stones. He'll breathe shallow at the stink of piss. He will see nothing at all as the light is gone, taken by the wind. He will feel it, cold on his face, as he hunches his shoulders, coughs.

Annie? Come away now . . .

Tommo will hear her breathing, sharp, each intake like a sob. He'll hear the scritching of her net against the bricks, a scuttle of tiny claws, the damp velvet dark pressing on his ears. And the sound. The *hooooing* of the wind, magnified now. And if Tommo puts his hand on the wall, presses his fingers into the grease and soot, he can feel the wall trembling, still. As if the coal train is coming.

Annie? I will make you a cup of black tea with sugar?

Slowly, Tommo's eyes will become accustomed, and magnify what light there is. Annie will be a shape in the darkness. She will come to Tommo like a bat, holding out the shrimping net.

Oh Tommo, can you reach up by there? Just there. I can see him, Tommo . . .

And he will hold her hand and scritch the net across the roof of the tunnel. The dirt will fall into Annie's upturned face, her threadbare donkey jacket. Dirt, soot, brickdust will all collect in Tommo's hair for he does not look up, oh no. Scritch. Scritch.

Maybe the wind will die down a little. The air in the tunnel will settle. Tommo will feel it, the air, it prickles, and the hairs on his neck rise to meet it.

Come on, love . . .

They'll walk back to her hut, Tommo's arm round her shoulders. Annie will have both hands on the net, like twin crabs holding it to her heart.

And when they reach the hut, she will go straight to the little fire just alive in the hearth. She will take the net from her breast, holding it closed with one hand. She will hold it out until it is right over the coals, right under the chimney open to the sky . . . and she will take her hand away, shake it, shake it.

She will sit on the stool by the warm, and smile.

My boy's in the chimney, Tommo, fetch the cup of water.

16

And Tommo fetches the thin white porcelain cup from the basket in the corner and fills it with water from the outside tap that rattles and chugs against the wall. And he gives it to Annie, not to drink, not at all; but to hold under the chimney for a mirror.

Is it going to be a moon tonight, Tommo? Will I see my boy?

Always happens, it does, regular as the church clock sticking at ten past the hour because of a nail. Then, Tommo in his suit walks back to the Savings Bank brushing the dirt from his hair, and leaves Annie talking to her chimney.

He passes by the steps of the cinema under posters with red lips, nods at a man as old as the century:

Hiya, Passchendaele

And chucks him a penny.

And Passchendaele Jenkins picks the penny out of his cap, holds it right up to his nose and squints at the head on the penny to see if it's a king. It isn't; not many of those around now. Only a queen.

He shakes that penny at Tommo like it's a fist because he remembers the day Batty Annie's living son went to play *Squash the King* in the railway tunnel, skipping school with a friend who didn't believe it could be done, and the tunnel still alive and yawning.

For a shilling Passchendaele Jenkins will sell his soul again and tell it to the cinema goers, counting Annie's son out like he's done a thousand times, wheeling his arms like the true Juggernaut and tapping the face of his watch with no hands:

17

Listen with your ears. I have a story for them see? About Batty Annie what lives now in the linesman's hut up by there. And her living son, Dai.

Making the bread in their house in Plymouth Street she was, when he had six minutes left only. Standing on a stool in the kitchen, reaching for the flour, they reckon, and her husband Evan coughing his guts out upstairs—but he still alive, just. Her Dai only seven. And she thinking he was at school, his dinnerpennies given in to the teacher, doing his sums to be a famous lawyer.

But he was not at school. Oh no. Tucked their satchels they had, behind the railway brickwork, him and Tommo Price, and only a shout or two away from his mother in her kitchen, there's the shame.

And she with the flour over the table, and the water, and the flour over her hands, and the water over her hands, and the softness of the bread gathering together, and the smell of the yeast, making bread for her men, him only seven and his Da who coughs his guts under the blankets at night until Mrs Pym next door rolls over Mr Pym in her curlers and bangs the wall.

'Is there no sleep to be had?'

See them now, the boys, sitting on the rail near the tunnel, eating cherry pip sweeties bought with Tommo Price's dinnerpennies, sticking their tongues out blood red down the middle. Their shoes fresh polished and shining like conkers for there was to be a singing for the real dead King at Ebenezer. Nice boys, both, in their school jumpers all tidy and straight. The one jumper machine-new and bought with money, the other made by Annie, full of love and knots.

Five minutes to go and they reckon Annie was up to the elbows in flour, softness under her nails, gathering it all together and rolling it away with her palms.

And Dai's talking about pennies. 'I can squash the King, Tommo.'

'No, you can't . . .'

'I can so, now then.'

And Tommo's pushing him, 'Nah, liar, you can't so there . . .'

'I can, so now . . .'

And Dai pokes Tommo in the side and he falls off his rail. Then they're up and running along the tracks they are, jumping the sleepers, hooooing like ghosts. Hooooooo into the mouth of the tunnel, and it hoooooos back at them, stretching like a waking dragon.

Four minutes and the coal train pulls out of Clydach, wheels spinning and sparking. With thirty trucks of steam coal. And the boys' shirts are loose, and their socks are round their ankles, and their shoes are dusty, look . . . and Annie's hair is in her eyes and she brushes it away with the back of a hand, and there's a streak of flour over her forehead like a message.

And her boy's fallen on the stones, he's hurt his knee all bleeding and his dinnerpennies have come out of his pocket in the half light. But he won't cry Oh no with his Da coughing at night and all and quite enough for his Mam to be going on with thankyou.

'I can squash the King, I can . . .'

But his best friend doesn't believe him and that matters.

'I don't believe you,' his best friend says, and oh, it matters. Dai's got his pennies in his hand now, off the ground where they were glinting. And it's three minutes and Dai who's never squashed the King says, 'The rails shift, see . . .' because he's heard the big boys talking in the street . . . 'The rails shift when the train's coming, Tommo. Up and down they go. Put the penny there too soon, it falls off . . .' And he thinks he sounds so knowledgeable, he does. Like an engineer.

'Have to wait, see. Have to wait 'til the train's nearly there.'

But Tommo says, 'Nah. You're scared, nah, the King won't squash like that, he won't.'

And they reckon it was two minutes when Annie saw Mrs Pym in the window opposite, waved, called her in to say sorry about the coughing with a cup of tea; a bit of hot water in the kettle and she put it on the gas, high. She could try Evan with one, give him two sugars for a treat. Went to the door in her pinny, stood talking, when her boy started his walk back into the tunnel.

'I will do it Tommo Price, you'll see . . .'

And Tommo Price put his hands on the brick walls and they were trembling.

'You will not.'

It was cold. Annie said to Mrs Pym that she'd go up to fetch a cardigan in a minute. 'Cold as the grave it is,' she said.

One minute and the rails were singing. The train was coming and its sound filled the tunnel and Tommo could not see the boy for the sound and the dark and he shouted to his friend, 'Come out!'

But the tunnel was so full of the sound of the train, the grinding and rattling, screeching and roaring, that his words were swallowed.

Passchendale will stop wheeling his arms and hug himself and he'll look at his watch with no hands, tap it and hold it to his ear where it ticks and ticks like a death watch beetle and never tells him anything other than that.

And him only seven . . .

Then cinema goers who have listened with their ears and their eyes—for they have followed the arms wheeling and the head rolling, and the eyes glancing up at the windows of the Savings Bank—want to finish the story.

Did he squash the King, bach bless him?

'I CAN SQUASH THE KING, TOMMO'

Oh did they find the penny then?

But the storyteller is off now, back begging he is, as the two o'clock is coming out all smiles and toffees.

~

The wind can be in any direction it likes and old Ianto 'Passchendaele' Jenkins in his khaki will always be begging on the steps of the cinema.

Film good was it? And the toffees? Oh that I had the teeth for a Callard and Bowser, now.

Mrs Prinny Ellis who takes the ticket money brings him a sandwich with beetroot. A welshcake. Yesterday's paper.

He has no bones, Passchendaele hasn't, mind, or he'd be stiff. No bones under them trousers.

Tommo Price can see Passchendaele from his window at the Savings Bank like God above who can do nothing once he's let his creation loose. He watches when people come out of the midday showing and stand with Passchendeale for aeons with him wheeling his arms and tapping his watch, and Tommo turns away and goes back to his ledgers. He drinks his tea from a thick cup and he fixes his eyes on his ledgers where the numbers stay still and solid and if he concentrates hard he only half hears his name.

Tommo Price it was. Tommo Price . . .

Tommo passes Passchendaele later on his way home from the Savings Bank and sometimes if he has the devil on his shoulder, Passchendaele waves a penny and *hoooooos* like the wind. Or a train.

Annie's son's in the chimney again, Tommo?

But of course there are no boys in chimneys, or in tunnels and Tommo Price goes home to Sarah Price who makes white fish for tea with white buttered bread and serves it silent. Lardy-faced, she is, and secrets slide away from her like dropped bulls eyes on a frozen puddle.

Aww. Off to Annie's now is it? There's a shame the fish is eaten all. Shame indeed.
You can tell me what she says, Tommo. I wouldn't breathe.
Indeed you wouldn't, my love.

Every night Tommo Price goes to Batty Annie's hut, just to make sure. Even when he is tired to the grave, like tonight, with watching the figures on the paper, and watching Passchendaele Jenkins on the cinema steps, looking up and watching him in return.

And tonight, this very night, the wind is blowing from the east and Tommo thinks to go straight to the tunnel where Annie will be as sure as eggs with her net. And she is not. It is past seven and the light is fading, and the tunnel is *hoooooing* soft and in waves.

Hoooooo ooooo

For a bit Tommo waits there, because she will come stumbling along any minute with her net. And he thinks of Annie there, waiting. The Annie who held him tighter once than his own mam and stroked and stroked his school jumper and left little dabs of bread flour and soft dough clinging to the wool and said it was not his fault.

But tonight, this very night, she doesn't come with her net. Tommo walks along the tracks to her linesman's hut and taps.

Annie?
Oh Tommo, there's a thing and I'm not very well . . .

And she is lying in the corner in her donkey jacket, not in the bed Tommo brought in pieces up the hill and nailed together again. Not under the blankets from his own cupboard.

Where's the coal, Annie? I will make you a nice fire, now, and some black tea with sugar.
Will you fetch my son, Tommo? I can hear him.

And Tommo gets Batty Annie onto the bed in her coat. He makes the fire, small, and sets the kettle on the coals, sighs and takes the shrimping net from up against the wall, and out he goes to the tunnel but he stands in the entrance out of the smell of piss and counts to one hundred swinging the net like a pendulum. And he goes back to the hut.

Where is he, my son?
Here, Annie, in the net . . .

23

Batty Annie listens.

He is not there Tommo. You don't have him you don't, my Lovely Boy.

So Tommo Price, who is tired from his day, bent over his ledgers and his white fish and his white wife, and finding Batty Annie ill, he goes back to the tunnel. And it's not like going back to stand in the tunnel with a net, but it's like going back to look for the penny like he did, over and over and not finding it, and kicking the stones around and piling them against the bricks, and clearing the ground to the mud and finding nothing at all. Because there was nothing to find. And he knew it.

All it ever was, was a boy who never *squashed the King*, killed by a train.

Tommo stands inside the tunnel and listens to the *hoooing* and does not lift the net. But he goes back tired to the hut holding the net like Annie does. Clasping it to his breast.

Here he is, Annie.

But she turns her face to the wall.

He's back in the tunnel, inside this time, inside the sound of the wind, inside the throat. There are blacknesses in the dark. And like he does for Annie, Tommo begins to scritch the net across the roof where the blacknesses are. Scritch scritch, and the old soot and the brickdust falls onto his face—for this time he is looking up. Scritch scritch. And he can smell the piss in the tunnel, and the damp and the dark, which smells like metal. The dark smells like metal. Like the warm damp fingers of a boy who's been clutching his dinner pennies, hard. Scritch

24

scritch. And it smells of sugar. Of cherry pips. And Tommo can taste cherry pips on his tongue like he hasn't for years, and knows that if he stuck his tongue out it would be red down the middle. And the soot and dust falls like black rain in the dark, a black rain that falls into the net and is heavier than dust.

Then Tommo feels in the net and finds that which is not dust. He holds it up in the half light, sees a face, and the face is flat, and he cries. He pushes it deep in his suit pocket and he cries. He scritches the net across the roof, fills the holes with darkness and the smell of pennies, and he cries.

Then Tommo holds his best friend to his breast, keeping the net shut against the closing night. But there's a moon up there, and it shines steady and unblinking down on the town and on Tommo Price taking Dai home to Annie along the old Merthyr coal line.

Tommo takes the net to the linesman's hut, straight to the hearth, and holds it out, right over the coals, right under the chimney, and he takes his hand away and shakes it, shakes it.

Then he takes the penny from his pocket and closes Annie's fingers round but he can't find the words to go with it.

He takes the white porcelain cup from the basket and fills it from the outside tap that rattles and chugs against the wall of the hut. He gives Annie to drink a little, slowly, holding the cup to her lips like it was a chalice. He takes a sip himself, then, knowing what he will see reflected in the water, he sits by the warm, leans forward, holds the cup out under the chimney and waits for the kettle to boil.

25

ON THE EDGE

I THINK I'VE just seen Smitz. Earl's Court tube, on his own, reading a paper. Must be ten years I haven't seen him. I watched him through the glass, through my reflection, waiting for him to tear that newspaper into little strips, walk to the edge, hold the strips up one by one in the underground wind, let them go. Maybe I should have yelled, banged on the window? Maybe I'll think about looking him up. We go back, Smitz and me.

The summer we turned thirteen, some do-gooder left money to give 'disadvantaged youths' a taste of fresh air and whelks. Our home, St George's, in some murky part of town, tipped us out into the Cornish sunshine. Like puppies tipped out of a box, blinking.

Thirteen. On the edge of something; Smitz closer to whatever it was than me. Puberty must've seen Smitz coming and ran at him like a train; it had missed me, Jez Harper, for the moment. Jez Harper was in a siding. But Jez Harper had worked life out. Worked adults out too. They like an easy life. They could fuck you up if you let them. Thing was not to let them know you knew that. Best thing was to get in first, fuck them up instead, quietly.

It wasn't Jez Harper's fault his mum died when he was five, or that his Dad buggered off before. I always try to remember that. Still fucked me up, both of them, didn't they?

I didn't speak for a month in my first foster home. I say I don't remember, but I do. It wasn't that I didn't have words;

26

just they went in instead of came out, burned a place in my stomach. When the words did come out they were blistering hot. I knew that, but they felt good. This woman was so stupid. Said she'd try to be like Mum for me, but how could she, she smelled different. I got cross, called her a stupid cunt. She cried so I called her it again. I lasted six months there. There were other places. Hot words still came out, some places were better about it. My stomach hurt. I didn't have a shit for a long time. I saw doctors; they gave me something to drink, three days running. I got cross, did it in my room at someone's house, on the floor. Why not? They said the room was mine. The shit was mine. If something's yours you can do what you like with it, right? I say I don't remember the shit, but I do. I say I don't remember making shit handprints on the wallpaper, but I do. I say I don't remember writing 'Jez' in shit over and over by my bed, but I do.

Smitz was at St George's already, been there three weeks. He was taller than me. He was OK. We had the same room, blue and red blankets. I wasn't much good at explaining why I was there. Smitz didn't seem worried, spilling his story after lights out my first night as soon as the squeak of rubber soles faded away up the corridor.

'My dad's Jamaican,' he said. His voice sounded like it was coming out of a tunnel.

I wanted to put the light back on. Smitz didn't *look* half Jamaican. He was tall, loose curls, dark skin that could be a suntan. I didn't say anything.

'Or, at least, he was.'

'Sorry.'

'I was three. I can just remember him, I think. Been in a few foster homes since.'

'Yeah. I was in those. Didn't work out.'

Smitz was quiet. Then, 'I called one of them 'Mum'. Just one, Sally. He was David; I never called him Dad. She had to go into hospital. I don't think she's coming home.'

I heard the slump of bedsprings as he turned over. His voice was muffled. 'Night.'

I was right about adults. Never get too close. They always dump you. I never asked about his real mum.

～

We shared a room on the holiday. Went places together. Smitz could piss from the harbour wall as far as the yellow buoy. We hung around drinking from a rusty tap, cans of coke, saving up our piss. We went crabbing, picked paint off upturned boats, poked sticks at dead dogfish, anything. All that water. Our stomachs were like footballs. If someone had swung at us, we'd've wet ourselves. We unzipped, counted ten, jigging so the piss was gagging to come out. We aimed, and on 'Ten!' pissed as hard as we could. Aimed so the arc wasn't too high, or you'd lose distance. My piss only went as far as the rust bucket the boat owners used to get to and from the jetty. But then Smitz had the advantage of a bigger dick.

Some people can't take a joke. Complained. That's why we went to Falmouth for the day on the bus with Jim, one of the carers. They gave us pocket money, a few quid. Said to stay in twos, be back at the bus stop by six. Jim was OK. I'd got him sorted. He was more interested in Clara, the girl he'd met at the pub last night. She just happened to be on the same bus.

We could have had a boat trip, shark fishing; that would have been good but we didn't have enough money. There was a

Dad taking two boys out, their Mum buttoning up their anoraks. I stood as close as I could to smell her, warm soap like after a bath. She kissed one boy on the head, and he pushed her off, said 'Mu-um,' like that. My stomach hurt.

We nearly went on a speedboat. It was red and black with silver trim; we wanted to go on that so badly. We queued up, a long queue, missed the next trip, stayed in the queue for half an hour in the sun, waiting, getting bored, joshing. Then the driver, a bloke in a tight blue tee shirt, wouldn't let us on. I said, 'Go fuck yourself if you can find yer dick.' A bloke with a stupid hat said to get lost. I called him a prick. In Woolworths we stood by the Pick 'n' Mix, knocked a few sweets on the floor, ate them. Some fat woman saw, told us to leave. I said, 'Go and get shagged if someone'll have yer.' We looked for interesting stuff, there wasn't any, and we had hours to go. Met one of the other guys in the street, and he said there was this joke shop up the hill.

'Pervy bloke. Good shop though.'

It was hot. It got hotter as we walked up the hill away from the water, looking for the joke shop. Shops and cafs then run-down shops and no cafs, then an old garage. Up the top, on the edge of town. A small park with broken railings. A row of joined up houses, a tatty launderette, its door open, breathing out more hot air, a sweet shop, newsagents. Then the place. It looked a good place. The windows were crammed with all sorts ... one side was all Dracula stuff, ghost stuff, plastic skulls, hands with nails through, spiders and bats on elastic, fake blood capsules, plastic teeth, broomsticks and black cloaks. It was all a bit collapsed in on itself, dusty, like no one had looked at it since last Hallowe'en. The other window had boxes of magic tricks, and some better stuff, fart sprays, bangers, fake dog turds, trick ciggies, trick soap, stink bombs. A box that said *Peppermint Penises.*

You kind of left the sun behind, going in. It took a time before your eyes got used to it. Funny thing was it smelled so familiar, like St George's. The Perve was there, sitting in an easy chair like he wasn't expecting too many people . . . behind the counter, an open door behind him. Couldn't see him properly at first. He was reading a magazine, holding it up close to his face. I could see why the others had thought he was a Perve. Too much, nearly in the dark. He smiled, and said 'Hi,' which was OK. He went back to his magazine. I reckoned dirty stuff, top shelf. Must've had his nose right up some woman, sniffing.

We spent ages just looking and joshing. It was good. Stuff was all under dusty glass counters, stuff we could afford, have some fun with. It was fun trying to decide what to get, who to 'get' with the stink bombs after lights out. Smitz and I were leaning on the glass, peering at the fart gas, adding up two of those, some bangers, fake ciggies, stinkbombs, packets of pellets that went 'crack!' on the pavement, and all the time this guy was breathing through his mouth. You could hear the breathing, too fast, like he'd been running. A click deep in his tubes. You could smell it. He let us josh about though.

We decided, got our money out, and the Perve got out of his easy chair. When he stood up the air in the shop smelled a bit of aftershave. He put the magazine down on the chair, came over.

'Right you are, boys.' He leaned on the counter, looking at us, so his face was close. 'Can I show you anything? Want to see something?' He was looking at Smitz, smiling. Dark hair greased straight back, pale blue eyes, face pitted like a battlefield. His skin was tight, shiny. His voice didn't go with the rest of him. It was a television voice. He was not that old. Wore a black jersey, even though it was so hot outside. His fingers fluttered on the glass, never kept still, like they were thinking about doing something else.

If I'd been Smitz, I'd have moved back. He didn't. He just held the guy's look like it was in his hands. Then he moved slowly, slow motion, liquid. He pointed out what we wanted, and the guy grunted, bent down to get things from under. I jumped up, leaned on the glass to see the mag, see a woman's bits.

Served me right. They weren't women. They were blokes. At least, you could see one bloke, white, and one big purple-black dick.

～

The others weren't at the bus stop yet. We walked down towards the boats again. The tide was right in. The shark fishing boat was empty, moored out in the river. It looked dead. The black and red speedboat was tied up too, further out in the channel, moving slowly, low in the water. The silver trims shone. It was almost silhouetted. There was no sign of the blue tee shirt or the daft hat.

'I'd have liked a ride on that,' Smitz said. 'Fast, wasn't it? Ever been on a speedboat?'

'Yeah, fast. Nah, never been on one. Fuck them. Blew it, didn't we? Fuck them.'

Smitz leaned on the railings, gazing at the boat. 'I reckon we could still swing it,' he said.

'Oh yeah?' I had picked up a few small stones from the gutter. I was lobbing them one by one as far as I could, watching them ping into the water. It was very still.

31

'If we had fifty quid I bet that bloke would take us out. Just us, if we had fifty quid. We could get him to take us straight out to sea, straight out where it's deep, and just keep going until we got to. . . .' He stopped.

'Where?'

'Somewhere.'

I looked at Smitz. I was thinking then of the scratches on our beds back at St George's, of scratching lines for months, bundles of five, crossed through for the sixth. Milestones.

'Where're we going to get fifty quid?' I said. 'Rob a bank?'

He didn't answer, but it was a not answering that said something.

~

It was easy to persuade Jim to take us back to Falmouth, next day. Clara came too.

'Meet you here at six,' he said when we got off the bus, and they went off towards the shops, arms round.

'You sure you're on for this?' Smitz said, as we walked up the hill.

'Yep,' I said. There was chewing gum on the pavement, round grey splodges. I wondered what it would taste like if you peeled it off and chewed it. It was sunny, breezy off the river. Smitz had showered, tarted himself up, put some oily stuff from one of the older guys on his hair. It smelt heavy. He'd got a white shirt on, the collar turned up. Denim jacket, the cuffs rolled back.

When we got to the park, Smitz ran his hands through his hair, brushing it back off his face. He looked older. He looked like someone had painted him. He pulled up his collar again, said, 'You wait here.'

He was gone. I had to notice things then. I had to look at things up close in the park, see things, remember them, fill my head with them. Green shiny paint on a bench where someone had tried to write a name. You can't write your name in thick gloss paint like that, it flakes. Dog shit on the path, a newspaper flapping. I picked up the newspaper, sat down on the bench. Bike tracks on the grass. The paper was crap, stuff no-one wants to read. They just buy it, throw it away. I tore the paper into tiny strips, listening to the paper tearing, tschhhk. I held the strips up in the breeze, let them go, seeing which would go farthest. It mattered that they should go a long way. I wanted them to catch the breeze. Some did. Some of them went up, curling on themselves then fell onto the grass. Some fell down straight away, until the path was white and grey with strips of paper. But I wasn't worried, I wasn't really watching what I was doing, I was looking at the black letters on the next strip, they didn't mean anything if you tore words up. I must've been hunched over, just tearing, tearing, tearing, throwing the things into the air.

Then there were Smitz's shoes on the path, in the paper strips.

'What the fuck you doing?' he said.

'I'm trying to get a piece of fucking newspaper to go up into the trees,' I said. 'What's it look like? It's not easy. What happened?'

Smitz fished in his jeans pocket. 'Twenty quid happened,' he said. 'He showed me his mag. I jacked him off. Let him jack me off.'

33

He sat down on the bench, bent down, picked up a handful of newspaper strips, started holding them up. They fluttered back down. He stood on the bench, held them higher. They caught the breeze better. Then we both stood on the bench, crowing like cockerels, letting newspaper ribbons fly round the park, all over the grass.

'What did you tell him?' I said.

'Said my friend was up for it. Said you'd be in later.'

I got the feeling Smitz wanted to go back near the river, so we went down the hill again, walking slowly, hands in pockets. We didn't talk much. The speedboat wasn't there. I got this idea it had sunk. It might have. If you leaned over the railings and stared at the water, the reflections burned the back of your head.

Later, I was walking back up the hill. I'd made him wait. Anyway, I figured less people would go up there late afternoon. Didn't want anyone coming in the shop, not with what I had to do. Smitz said the Perve had turned the sign to 'closed' and they'd gone through the curtain into the back, that's where it had happened. I said to Smitz I wanted to go on my own, but he followed me. He flipped sideways into doorways if I turned round, so I just kept on walking. My running shoes on the pavement sounding like a dog panting.

There were still a few bits of newspaper in the park, flapping on the grass, caught round the legs of the bench. It was getting cold. The sun was round the back of the houses.

The door shut. I didn't say anything, just stood there. The Perve was on a chair, reaching up, putting something on a shelf. He looked down. Grinned. I grinned back.

'I'm Jez.'

'Hello, Jez.'

34

~

I found Smitz in the park. He was sitting on the green bench, picking at the paint with his thumb, chewing at the inside of his cheek. I sat down, stretched my legs out, waited for him to say something first. He didn't.

'OK?' I said.

Smitz took his two crumpled tenners from his pocket, held them between us on the bench with his finger. He'd been biting his nails. I fished in my pocket, lifted his finger, took the notes. I put them on the path, held them down with my shoe.

Then I fished in my own pocket, brought out two twenties and a ten, handed them to Smitz.

'Fifty.' I said.

Smitz looked at me then. 'Was it OK? What did he want you to do?'

I thought for a bit. 'All sorts,' I said. Smitz looked away.

I picked up his money, got up, stood on the bench. Started tearing one of his tenners into tiny pieces, chucking them over Smitz like dandruff, like confetti. Then the breeze took some, blew them around. Smitz didn't speak, looked up, shading his eyes, blinking. Smitz never cried.

'C'mon up,' I said. 'It feels fucking good tearing up money.'

I stood there, tearing up that tenner, letting the bits fly around. The smaller they were the better they flew around. Then I told him.

'He wanted all sorts. Blow job. Had a camera. I didn't *do* anything. Got him excited, then said I'd go to the Fuzz. Dunno how much he gave me to get the fuck out.' I pulled out a fistful of crumpled notes, then shoved it all back in my pocket. 'See?'

35

Smitz nodded, wiped his nose on his sleeve. Then he climbed up, and tore that other tenner up like his life depended on it.

~

The wind in our faces. The tight blue tee shirt bloke driving us like we were the tops. Just Smitz and Jez. We bounced over the waves in that red black silver speedboat, slapping the water. We held on, said 'fuck, fuck . . .' turned round and watched the coastline getting smaller. Houses getting smaller, bleeding together.

I looked ahead of us, at the horizon. It was clear blue. A few sailing boats. I thought you just don't know, do you? You don't really know if there's something beyond the horizon. Just because people tell you, doesn't mean there's anything there. It could be just a line. Maybe when you look over the edge the air is chocca with people falling, falling. You just feel there must be *something*, though, so you don't ask. The boat bounced over a wave, slapped down hard. White water hit us, salt, cold. Shock.

Then Smitz started laughing. And I started laughing. We couldn't stop. And the horizon just got bluer. I thought of the park. I looked back to see if I could see it, but I couldn't. I leaned back, closed my eyes, felt the wind in my hair, and thought of bits of paper flying round the park, all over the grass, covering the dog shit, like a wedding.

36

BONES

LIKE A GREAT gaping mouth full of teeth it is, he said, my Dad.
Like great tombstones of teeth sticky out every which way, he
said. He was right. Had to pay to go in, though, but that made
it special somehow. Like you had to concentrate more to get
your money's worth.

We went to the synagogue too. Had to buy one of those hats,
made of paper it was, and he didn't like that, my Dad, he said
bloody hell look, who do they think I am, but I said just put it
on, OK. So he did.

It was lovely in there. It was dead peaceful, sort of thing, and
I could have sat and watched the dust circling, and felt ever so
you know. But Dad, a quick look round and he said he'd had
enough. What, I said, even with those kids singing. And they
were too. Singing. No one told them to, they just sang, and it
sounded strange coming out of their mouths like that. Old
music. Really old. And ups and downs in it that were like another language. I suppose that's what got to my Dad. He
doesn't speak languages. Thinks everyone ought to speak his,
sort of thing. But I said, hang on there Dad, just listen. It's lovely
isn't it? But he'd taken off the paper hat and screwed it up by
then so we had to go.

The sound of those boys' voices sort of came out with us.
Like it was in our pockets. Music in our pockets, funny that.

Then we crossed the road to the cemetery. Have we got to go in here, he said, and I said of course we have, Dad you're supposed to see this when you're here. And it was beautiful. Those tombstones like giant teeth, all crazy, on soil piled so high it looked like the sea, and waves of bodies trying to swim up to the surface. There's fifteen layers of bodies there, they said. Fifteen layers.

They closed the cemetery well before Kafka walked round here. Oh yes, he would have seen this. SEEN THIS. And Dad couldn't care less.

There's this one stone, Rabbi someone, who was dead important, sorry that sort of came out wrong, but I know, and he probably knows what I mean to say. And you could go right up to the stone, leaning like the Tower of Pisa only smaller. There were people putting pebbles on the top. Little ones, Finding pebbles from the earth and balancing them on top and I wanted to cry. But Dad said what's the matter with you, girl? Like that. So when he'd gone on a bit, and was grouching near the exit, I said I'd dropped something. What? he said. Anything, I said over my shoulder and I ran back, saying excuse me, through the line of people coming round, because it's all one way. And I found a small pebble. It was fallen off another gravestone, but I didn't reckon it would matter really. And I went to the Rabbi's stone, and stood with this old chap. God he was old; he was dead old, but not dead, sort of thing, but he looked as though he could have been. And it was funny, we both leaned forward at exactly the same time, and put our pebbles on top of the grave. And we sort of smiled. He could see I wasn't Jewish, I think, but he didn't seem to mind.

He smiled at me, and I could sort of see Dad saying don't smile at strangers, Mags, but there you are. This man looked sort of sad, and old, and all I did was smile.

Then there was Dad at the exit in such a mood. We've got to go up these bloody stairs now, he said. Why the hell can't we just get out? It was a narrow stairs, one way again, and Dad complaining, and holding on to the banister too long. Where are we going now, he said. But it was dead nice up there. There were all these drawings, like school kid's things, sort of what I would have done a few years ago. Crayons, and pencils, drawings of people, stick people, schools, flowers, and lots of drawings of people holding hands and smiling. There were words too, big letters in crayon, lots of them faded. I couldn't make them out, and went to ask Dad what they said. But he'd gone all quiet. And waved me away. So I walked round the room to see if I could fathom it out. Lots of old luggage labels, and a cracked leather suitcase in a glass case. Lots of passport photos. But no grown ups. All kids. Like me. And I thought I'd better ask Dad now. And I went over, but he had his head against the wall, and was not speaking.

I read about this story by Kafka, last night in the hostel. I don't understand it, but I'm going to try again, maybe next year. *The Trial* it was called. Dead good, probably. This guy he doesn't know what he's on trial for exactly. It just happens. And no one does anything about it.

Sort of like these kids really.

And it was even more dead funny because when we came out, Dad was blowing his nose on a handkerchief, and I was embarrassed because it echoed on the stairs. And all these people looked round. When we got out you could still hear the singing. Those boys singing, just sort of floating down the street.

And this time, my Dad sat on the kerb, right outside the cafe on the street next to the synagogue, he sat on the kerb, with people walking all round him and making sort of Oh look at that daft man faces, and he looked up at me and said 'Listen, Mags. Listen to that. It's beautiful.'

SMOKING DOWN THERE

KATH SAID SHE had a brother she rescued from a bucket of water.

But then Kath said lots of things. She said she knew how to make a shoe float on the river and come out dry and unsunk. She said she knew how to smoke two cigarettes at once. Between her legs.

I knew that all that was tosh. You couldn't get shoes to float on the river. Not this one. It was fast and full of waves; it ran over stones close to the surface.

Kath said her mum had gone into labour when they were staying with her Nan. Early. That she'd wanted to go up the hospital but they wouldn't take her. That Mrs Douglas with the wall eye was called in instead, because she 'did' all the babies in Jehova Street.

I was more interested in the cigarettes. How could you breathe in between your legs? But I wasn't going to ask. Anyway, how did she know? I saw a film once where a cowboy sat by a waterfall and blew smoke rings before killing his best friend. Could you . . . ?

The houses in Jehova Street were joined up, Kath said. Like a kid's handwriting, with dark alleyways between every fourth one. Kath's Nan had four bolsters jammed up against the bedroom window so the neighbours wouldn't hear the screams.

41

That was Mrs Douglas. Said if the neighbours got meithered, the baby'd be cursed, and she wasn't having that.

I reckoned, when you were grown up, you could just about hold a cigarette between your bottom lips. But. You couldn't walk around with it in there. So what was the point?

Kath said she was downstairs playing marbles on the kitchen floor. With sloes from the tip. The tiles were old and uneven, and the bloody sloes (she swore a lot) kept gathering in one line near the table leg. So she got cross and smashed them. She'd never done that before, and expected dark blue juice.

She could hear the screams. It sounded like three cats on a wall, she said, not her mum. She said she'd never smash a sloe again. It looked like blood on the tiles, and what happened next was probably because of the curses put on the sloes by the travellers.

I guessed, too, that if you did smoke down there, you'd have to take it out when you went to bed.

Silence.

Kath said she could hear her own heart beating like it had been switched to her outside and plugged in. Creaking floorboards. Didn't want to look up at the kitchen ceiling in case there was blood coming down the walls and that'd be the end of her pocket money. Mercenary, was Kath. And she had a black plait I never saw undone.

She said she counted 100. Fast. And the quiet and the creaking just got quieter and more creaky. And maybe she was making it all up, because maybe she'd been ill and just woken up and it was all a dream.

She said there was a brown velour curtain over the door to the front room which had three cigarette holes near the bottom. Velour melts if it's cheap, she said. But she still went and hid behind it because sound carried down the stairs to the front room.

Nothing. Not even breathing.

Then Nan came down all red-faced with her hair sticking out of her hairnet, and only one shoe. Rushed out the back door, came in with a bucket of water. Back up stairs, shoulders all askew.

That, Kath said was the funny bit. She said that you needed to wash down there a lot when you were grown up because it got hairs, and because dirt clung to the hairs. But then, if you smoked down there why didn't the hairs catch fire? That's what I wanted to know. But the bucket. Why wash out of a bucket when there were perfectly nice china things?

So she waited for the creaks again, and went up stairs, matching her footsteps on the steps to the creaks.

And, at the top of the stairs, there was the bucket, outside the bedroom door. Closed. And the pale bottom of a pair of little feet under the water. And a pale bottom. Upside down. Huge boys bits showing. Purple under the water.

Kath picked up the bucket and could hardly. . . . And the water was right to the top, slopping down the stairs, and she got the bucket to the kitchen and tipped it up on the tiles and this little boy slopped and slid onto the floor with the sloe juice. And she said that she knew you were meant to slap babies on the back

43

but there wasn't much point with this one. (Like she'd seen hundreds. See what I mean about telling fibs?)

There wasn't much point because he had a bit of skin all over his face. Just thin. Like rice paper under buns. And his face had gone in the sloe juice. She said she'd cop it something chronic now, so she got the floor cloth and wiped the baby's face.

Now, you see, when we left that school at eleven, and before I never saw her again—only a few times, as she moved away—she told me that the trick with the shoes in the river was to get four balloons. Put the shoe in one, blow up the others and tie them on so it holds the shoe up. And the one it was in kept the shoe dry, and safe.

I met her brother once. Gareth. He came with his Mum to a play Kath and I were in. Looked just like her, too.

I tried smoking a cigarette down there much later. It didn't work.

IRRIGATION

THE THINGS WE do to ourselves. Shelley's lying in someone's
front room with a large plastic tube up her bum. Serbian Vera
sterilises everything as soon as poss after, so she says. You just
have to trust people.

'Oh, you that poor, poor, poor lady from fifteenth floor?'
Serbian Vera said when Shelley called by.

'Leave it out.' Shelley said.

You don't sterilise everything, apparently. Some stuff you
chuck. There are throw-away bits, like the bit that's up there at
the moment. It's funny really—Shelley's never spoken to
Serbian Vera before although they've lived twenty-eight feet
apart for six years, not as the crow flies, more as the cockroach
scrabbles. That's what Shelley calculated when the tube was
going up, although it didn't hurt really, it was just uncomfortable, more in her head than anywhere else.

Three floors down; twenty-eight feet. Serbian Vera's on the
twelfth. Shelley wonders if sound carries down or up or both, if
when things were OK and she and Pete went at it like rabbits
people like Mrs Patel upstairs heard, or the man in the vest
next door with the guinea pigs, or even Serbian Vera. But she
hasn't said anything.

Pete's gone now, sort of. *He's* gone, but he's still in Shelley's
head. Years of someone like Pete don't just go when his voice
has gone. That's what Shelley knows; she's been waking up at

three thirty and just listening to her head, Pete's words flinging round in her skull. Why can't Shelley remember nice words? And why couldn't people hear the nice things he said? Because he did.

This all started at SupaSaver, standing by the notice board, Shelley working out if she could afford a cooked chicken, and seeing this postcard saying Serbian Vera was qualified and did irrigations in her front room. Down the library Shelley sat next to a wino and looked up *colonic irrigation* while the wino stink settled round her head.

But she found out all sorts. That colonics flush pints and pints of warm water round your guts and everything old and stale comes away. She'd crouched forward in her seat with her hands over her belly and the wino'd said, 'Are you OK?' which was nice.

Shelley said, 'Oh. Yes thanks, I'm fine, sorry,' then wondered why she'd said sorry. Habit.

That's neat though, the thought of doing work in your front room. Maybe Shelley'll set up a hairdressing salon when all this with Pete is over? You can get loads of stuff cheap enough, and so long as people don't ask for extensions, which are a pig, or too much red in the colour, because that's the hardest to get right, it could work. And so long as people don't ask for qualifications, because Shelley left the Tertiary when she met Pete— but she didn't miss much, everyone said.

Shelley's remembering Pete's mouth. Chipped front tooth. The way his lip caught on that tooth. The way his hair made a bird's nest at the back in the mornings, his laugh. Used to laugh a lot, once. Easy to love, Pete was. A big kid, made Shelley rip her sides, didn't he? Like a naughty little lad.

46

He'd say things like, 'Hey Shell, found these in Garfield's,' and hold out a handful of gold chains, earrings, a watch. He'd grin. And that tooth would catch again. He'd order breast of chicken dhansak and spinach bhajee and spicy poppads down at the Bombay Culinary Experience and when they'd finished, pull Shelley up and say they were friends of the owners . . . then run.

Serbian Vera's saying something about being what we eat, and Shelley's thinking we're probably what we love, too. You can't just switch love off, can you? Serbian Vera's going on about food that gets stuck inside, in all the little folds and things and she's saying it as though it's gold nuggets ready for panning.

Shelley talks a bit too fast, says, 'But we get used to eating stuff, then the recipe changes in the packets and we don't bother to look. So what was OK for us ends up being bad for us, all because we didn't keep our eye on the packets. Bad, isn't it?'

Serbian Vera looks like Shelley's mum did. Permed hair, brown, with a white rosette growing out round a split crown. Shelley might suggest a tube of that Harmony Highlights in Warm Chestnut because Serbian Vera's brown is too like a wig. Maybe when she knows her a bit better. But it's not easy to keep up the chat with someone from Serbia whose English sounds like something off The Sound of Music heard through a wall. Also, how can you know anyone better than when they've just parted your bum cheeks with rubber gloves and stuck a white plastic thingy up your bum?

'Rrrelax, please,' Serbian Vera says and flippers her tongue on the roof of her mouth when she says it. Shelley's lying on her side on this collapsible table thing covered in white towels, nose almost up against the wallpaper which is a green trellis with dripping mauve roses. She tries flippering her tongue too, makes a funny noise. 'And you allrright?' Serbian Vera says, 'You lie on the back, now.'

Shelley shifts onto her back, knees up like when the doctor sent her to the Gynae, and Serbian Vera puts a white cot blanket over her belly, then checks everything underneath.

'Has it started yet?' says Shelley and thinks about anal sex. Pete wanted that, once he was on the skunk. Oh that stuff changed him right through. Weed seemed OK but skunk? God. Turned him onto all sorts. Said he couldn't do it the other way because of the bump, it made him gag. Got her doggy once on the settee while Match of the Day was delayed, Shelley leaning on her arms, face near that cigarette burn in the burgundy velour. And she watched the burn while Pete fingered her and said she looked like a horse from the back. She thought about moths. About whether moths eat nylon velour or whether it's just real stuff they go for, but then her face was pushed into the cushions. It hurt. Then Pete called her a fucking slag when she said it wasn't good for her, then the teams were coming on and Shelley went to soak in the bath with the door locked and told herself it wasn't Pete, wasn't Pete, just the skunk and when he didn't do it any more, the skunk, that things'd be OK. Maybe, maybe if she loved him a bit harder, things'd be OK?

'It start now,' says Serbian Vera, and for a bit Shelley can't feel anything at all. Then it's warm just a bit in her belly, low down, and Serbian Vera's hand is on Shelley's Caesarean scar. She peeks under the cot blanket and doesn't ask, because probably she's thinking where is baby now, then?

Shelley says, 'He was a big baby.' But Serbian Vera's not looking at her and Shelley won't explain anything. Not with this tube up her bum she won't.

48

Oh. Now it's like she has to shit herself. Oh. Shit. Shelley squeezes her bum tight round the plastic thing and it's building up and up in her belly like a dam going to break. She's getting ready to say sorry but Serbian Vera says, 'Is fine, just let go,' and she doesn't need to be told that because she can't help it, there's a warm rush like the squits out of her bum.

'Oh my GOD, I'm so sorry,' Shelley says, shutting her eyes and waiting for the smell.

'Well done, lady,' says Serbian Vera and she's watching the machine on the sideboard next to a white china swan. There's a photo frame on the machine: a man with a moustache. He's wearing a uniform. Shelley wonders what he thinks of being balanced on a poo tube. She's still looking at the machine, and there's a clear plastic tube bit with a procession of shit going left to right like Notting Hill Carnival.

It's like being a baby again, must be; there must be a memory far back somewhere—lying here shitting and not worrying. Letting it all go. Like baby Declan did for a few months. There are tears coming behind Shelley's eyes, but she won't cry. Pete hated shitty nappies, said they stank. But they didn't. Baby shit doesn't stink. Not like adult. Not like Pete's did when he crapped himself on the velour settee when he got pissed on Stella and all that smoking. He'd pissed himself before and Shelley could smell it on the air, sort of a green smell, heavy. Not like this. Awful. It stank the place out and all he said was, 'Thank Christ I wasn't at Brian's or there'd have been a real fight,' and he'd gone to get some more skunk off his contact and left the shit to Shelley.

Down the library the book said there was this bloke had an irrigation in Thailand in 2001—had a blue marble come out of his bum. Shelley thinks that's absolutely amazing. Out of his bum. A blue marble. Turned out he'd swallowed it in 1974 to stop his brother getting it. Fuckin' Ada. The book didn't say if he took the marble home, or what.

Shelley wants to ask Serbian Vera about things that may be going down the tube. Before she does, Serbian Vera says, 'Here, look. All healthy,' and she swivels the machine round so Shelley can take a good look at her own shit procession. Mmmm. Nice.

Now her belly's tightening again, sort of contracting. 'Another lot coming,' says Serbian Vera, 'wait for it,' but there's no need to tell Shelley—she's getting used to it now, the squits building up and up and up then ooooh with a rush. Next time she's going to watch her stomach. See if it goes up and down like a balloon.

'Who's that in the photo?' says Shelley.

'My husband,' says Serbian Vera. 'He dead now in Serbia,' and she sort of brings the drawbridge up. So Shelley doesn't ask any more about the man in the photo for now.

Shelley asks if they do colonics in Serbia and Serbian Vera says, 'They might now but not back then. Was a war on. No colonics in war.' Then she says, 'O look,' and stares at the tube, and Shelley says, 'What?' There's a line of what looks like little brown moles going for a walk. 'My god—is maybe dead mouse,' says Serbian Vera.

'What do you mean, dead mouse?' says Shelley, half sitting up but Serbian Vera's got out of her chair and says, 'My god, if I could stop machine I would show it. You have mice in flat?'

'No,' says Shelley, 'I don't and anyway that can't have been a mouse because it'd be all digested wouldn't it?'

'Depends,' says Serbian Vera. 'Depends if it hide in the folds. You get all sorts in folds and things.'

Shelley wants to get up but she can't and she almost wants Pete back but thinks nope, that's just habit, Shelley. Serbian Vera's looking pale. Maybe she's a nutter? But somewhere in Shelley's head she feels sorry for the mouse, if it was a mouse, in case it was a mouse. Like she was given something tiny and ever so precious to look after, but people forgot to tell her.

'How did your husband die?' says Shelley.

'I have three people tell me three things,' says Serbian Vera. 'Number one: he hero. Number two: he bully shot by own men. Number three: nobody knows where he die. I choose number one.'

Shelley looks at the photo. It doesn't tell her much. You can't say much about dead husbands, dead mice, dead babies, even to nutters. Mind you, nice to be able to choose in your head like that.

Shelley's wondering what it's like not really knowing though. Not having a body. Because even they had Declan's body. After they'd taken him away and done tests and stuff and called it unexplained infant mortality or something like that. But somewhere deep inside, Shelley knows better. Can't get rid of this dream she has where Pete is smiling and holding a dirty pillow over the cot. Maybe she made that up? Not sure.

They brought Declan up all those floors by the stairs because the lifts were broken. Brought him up to spend the last night at the flat, like they'd said would be a good thing. Shelley in the kitchenette, windows locked. She'd have liked to open the window but she'd lost the key, or Pete had. Can't remember. Doesn't matter. These two blokes came all the way up the stairs and rang at the bell and said, 'Where d'you want him love?' like he was a delivery from Tesco's.

Shelley said, 'In the kitchen, please' and they stuck this white box on the Formica and hung about. Shelley thought maybe they hung about for a tip.

And the bigger bloke said could he use the loo and she hadn't wanted an undertaker using her loo so said, 'It's blocked.'

There were clouds in the shape of monkeys with sticky out ears. And one big one like a boat over the gasometer. And the smell of the flowers, heavy round her head like someone in thick white gloves was pushing your face in so you couldn't breathe. And Pete came in and said he couldn't breathe either, and he'd been doing stuff like skunk only more, what, crack or whatever because that's what the lads were into now. In and out of their heads, in and out of trouble.

Serbian Vera says, 'Come back, darling,' and she's patting Shelley's belly and saying, 'You got yourself a nice flat tummy.'

'Thanks,' Shelley says, who is shitting again and saying, 'Jesus, there can't be MORE in there, can there?'

'No, it mostly water now,' says Serbian Vera, but Shelley can see it's got little dark flecks in like specky tar. And the odd sultana. Shelley had sultanas yesterday in the rice from a Bombay Culinary Experience take away. Still can't go and eat in there.

'What's that tar stuff?' asks Shelley.

'Oh, not tar,' says Serbian Vera, 'very old bits now, difficult bits, stuff is stuck in folds.'

'Oh, like the mouse,' says Shelley.

'Maybe,' says Serbian Vera, not smiling.

Pete tried to open the window. Said, 'Fuck me, Shell, I can't breathe with all these fucking flowers,' and he'd got up on the draining board. High as a kite. And something inside Shelley just removed the flats. In her head she saw Pete on the draining board, herself with dirty hair and on an important day too, Declan in his white box just floating inside a steel girder skeleton up in the sky. No dripping manky concrete. And Pete was working at the window with something. A jemmy. Something. Saying, 'I can't breathe. Deccy can't breathe, can he?' Working at the metal window until it bent. Opened.

He jumped down into the kitchen—bang—off the draining board and picked up Declan's white box, climbed back again. Shelley didn't want to touch the white box. Because if she touched the white box Deccy might put a hand out of the wood and grab her tee shirt.

'I can fly, Shell,' Pete said.

Shelley was feeling exactly like you do when you're on the platform in the tube and the train's coming; you can sort of half hear it, and you know it's coming because of the wind. Warm and gentle and safe—saying it'll be OK—the wind telling you the train's coming, love.

Serbian Vera's saying, 'OK, all finished. I take the tube out and you hold on, OK, the loo is over there. You go straight and sit on, OK?' So Shelley does. She sits on and shits water looking at a knitted loo roll holder like a white poodle. Loads of water. Waterfalls. When it's finished she looks at it between her thighs and it looks bitty. Black bits again. And it smells sweet, just like Declan's nappies.

53

'You OK, Shelley?' says Serbian Vera through the door. But Shelley's not OK, because she's sitting on the loo looking at more green trellis wallpaper with drippy mauve flowers and she knows that somewhere in all the folds and chinks inside you there are always more black bits. That all the water in the world won't wash Pete away. That we are what we love, not what we eat. That when Pete was saying, 'I can fly,' on the draining board and she was standing there wanting to pull their Declan's little white box away from him, that she had a choice. Like what Serbian Vera chose to believe.

She could say, 'Don't be a daft fucker, Pete, come down, put Deccy down,' or she could say, 'Yes Pete, you can fly. Show me.'

EXCAVATION

'MALE, SIX-FIVE-eight-zero?'

'Yes.'

'You know why I'm here?'

'Yes. Will this hurt?'

She kneels beside me, runs her eyes over me, speed-reading. Her voice softens.

'No. It won't hurt. I promise you that.'

This is what they do now. They send one of these personal archaeologists to plumb you before you die. To excavate your hidden places, dig through the scar tissue; to lay bare and gasping things that haven't breathed for years, before you snuff them out. I lay on the bed, naked, little bloodless trenches all over, my archaeologist kneeling at my side. She runs her finger between my nipples, winding her fingertips in my chest hair, pulling it gently. She runs the finger down over my sternum. She pauses it above my navel. She is watching her hands. They are small, square, purposeful hands, slim fingered, short nailed, the backs are freckled. Some of her fingers are calloused at the tip, I can feel them, tiny, dry and scraping over my skin like so many arthritic spiders.

She kneels over me. It would not take much for this to be another place, another time, and she, paid, pretending interest in these bones. She is young, small, lithe. Her fingers work fast.

55

Her hair, undefined, wispy, tied back but escaping, looks like straw. She has small even teeth, at least, mostly even. I like mouths. They have told me, taught me a lot. This mouth is relaxed, generous, unthinking. The one uneven tooth catches inside her top lip. She moistens the lips to slide them over the unevenness. There is something heartbreaking about that mouth, about the action. Her face is fine featured, intelligent. Unplucked eyebrows over grey eyes. Almost expressionless, she has remained for hours working in and over my body. Only the eyes have moved, flickered, shadows passing over them like the wind ripples the surface of the sea. Those lips have moved, speaking my body away into her microphone.

Now, her hand moves over my belly and she cups me gently. 'Have you always been kind, I wonder?' she says, not looking at me at all, holding me. I feel my skin contract, shiver.

'I feel kindness,' she says, her head lowered slightly, her voice disappearing. 'I feel kindness,' she says again, disbelieving, looking up at my face now. I try to smile.

There *has* always been kindness. Never anything less. Sometimes more, but maybe she has not plumbed that. I have not raped. I have paid, sure, but they were always women, not things. Always people, not ciphers. Always a girl, a woman with as much need as I. Different, but as much.

She pushes her fingers underneath the skin at the top of my thigh, bloodless, painless. 'I wonder why?' she says, almost to herself.

Why? I close my eyes. There are so many, many answers. Because I have loved. Because I liked. Because I needed. Because I was so sad I thought I might never resurface. Because I needed company. Because the solitude of living in this body might have been enough to finish me were it not for the warmth of sliding into another. It reminded me I was alive, sometimes.

I am erect. She ignores me, feeling beneath my skin, closing her eyes, relying on touch. I feel the movement, small scrape of callous, the probe of her flesh. Her eyes snap open. 'I have you,' she says. 'Just once. There are adhesions. Did you know?' Scar tissue that runs from groin to lung, which tugged at me for years, which stopped any other woman coming close. I do not speak, but my eyes have filled. She takes out her fingers, and leans over me. 'I'm sorry,' she whispers. 'I have to collate . . .'

She kneels up, and leans over me, both hands now flat on my chest. She is weightless, like a bird. I can see small blonde hairs on her upper lip. The lip has dried again, the single tooth catches it. I want to moisten it for her. She catches me looking at her mouth and runs the tip of her tongue over her lip, pulling it back against the lower. She smiles, her lips slicked, small, her jawbone fragile, as though I could crush it between my fingers.

'Here,' she says, rubbing the tips of her fingers below my left nipple. 'We are nearly done. This will be the last excavation.' Her eyelashes are tiny straw spikes. Her eyes are grey. Pale grey like clouds.

She has done well. We don't hear much about these excavations, only hearsay. They collect the body's imprints, the buried memories deep in the tissue and bone. The torn, broken and mended. The invasion of disease, the counterpoint of serum. All those life prints left in us like so many fading impressions on sheets of paper beneath a letter.

She has collated my body, spoken it into her microphone. Joining it to a million others. There is not room for us all to live

57

late, like they used to. We have bartered health for longevity, planning and collation for a spontaneous end.

She straddles me, excavating my heart. Her small fingers move inside my chest, lifting, feeling, palpating. She speaks into her microphone. The words begin to blur, to fade. I can no longer catch the whole, but the gist. 'A good man . . . kind, who has loved only once.'

'No, not just the once,' I say, forcing the words up and out from where I am drowning. My little archaeologist finishes her whispering, and sits back. She lifts herself, bends forward to my mouth, her small tooth caught again. This time I moisten her lip as she slides onto me.

'I wish . . .' she says.

DODIE'S GIFT

THERE IS A little blood on the sand, in a hollow in the dunes. There is semen too, although it is hidden in the shadows where sand and grass have been churned. The blood is clear, scarlet, bright; both its colour and its brightness out of place in the soft grey-green and pale straw colours here. It will fade soon, darken until it's almost black, and it will be lost when a herring gull chooses this place to bring the head of a newly dead catfish. He will drop it, stand over it, stabbing at it with his yellow hooked beak, parting skin from muscle, lip from cheek, eye from socket, until all that is left is a mess of reddened bone and one thin sliver of catfish skin with a feeler still attached.

There are tracks leading in different directions. One set, Dodie's, scramble up the side of the dune, the sand puddled and broken where she tried to claw her way out of the hollow, the top slipping further away with every step. The marram grasses are crushed where she slid down towards the field. The barley stubble is also crushed, over, over, over, where Dodie ran crying to the General Stores.

The other footmarks are The Philosopher's, weighted, regular, the sand only disturbed and uneven in one spot at the base of the slope where he stood to adjust his clothing before striding away towards the caravan site.

~

Who is Dodie? Just this: a woman in her forties who works at the Stores. Invisible. She wears a blue nylon overall, and if it is hot she is uncomfortable by the end of the day. Maybe she smells of onions. She sleeps above the Stores in a small room that overlooks the yard. She's worked here as long as the surfers and body boarders who stay at the caravan site can remember. If you find her at the Tinner's Arms in the evening, you'll see she doesn't drink much, makes half a cider last all evening, but Bill at the Tinner's doesn't mind. She's a fixture who has a place here, whereas in a city she would drown.

It is difficult to give a name to what makes Dodie different. There is no lack of intelligence, with her appetite for reading of all sorts, crosswords, number puzzles. But it is as though a membrane separates Dodie from the world. As though she was born covered in a cowl which was never quite stripped away. She looks at you, puzzled, trying to work you out, trying to read you, know you.

What she does know is here, in the Stores. She knows the pastel and black plastic tops of deodorants and the gold, white and green of hairsprays. She knows the sugary smell of Lux soap, the deeper elusive scent of Imperial Leather. She knows the jolly primary colours of perfect cereal bowls on the packets of own brand and Kellog's. She knows how sticky soap powder feels if it spills out of the box.

Dodie reads everything. Everything that comes in to the Stores in twine-tied bundles brought by the paper van. Newspapers. Women's magazines, white smiles on the cover, *How to cook for six on a shoestring. Sex after the menopause? It's great!* Men's magazines with bottoms and breasts pushing out on the front cover. Children's comics. Puzzle books. She uses the photocopier in the back to copy the puzzles. Fishing periodicals.

Surfing magazines. Music magazines. The special stamp-collecting issue that comes in for Mr. Fisher next to the Church Hall. She takes them up to her room and reads them all, careful not to mark them, then pushes them under the mattress to flatten them and puts them on the shelves the next day.

Who is The Philosopher? Just this: a man in late middle age, like a million others, greying, spreading, unremarkable. Invisible, too. He came into the General Stores towards the end of a day in mid-September, and stood by the bread racks. He put one hand up to a Mother's Pride plastic wrapper, and just stood there, head bowed, his rucksack making it difficult for other shoppers to pass easily. Dodie waited for a while before coming out from behind the counter.

'What are you doing?' she said, glancing at his face, then away.

The man looked up at the bread, then at her. 'I'm thinking,' he said. 'I'm thinking about bread.'

'OK, but could you think over there?'

The man did not smile, although his eyes narrowed a little and it could have been a smile coming. Dodie had read that smiles start with the eyes. But if she had looked closer, there were no laughter lines. He took a loaf of bread and moved to the till. Dodie took his money without a word. From then on he was, to her at any rate, The Philosopher.

~

They know little about each other after a few days of him appearing in the Stores, standing there, thinking. He chooses his times. Chooses times when the Stores isn't too busy, so he can stand and think. Because he knows it intrigues her.

She has no idea who he is. Just a man, slightly overweight, staying on the caravan site (she asked), cheap deal, last minute. Caravan sleeping four, but he's only one. He goes for long walks, alone. She's seen him in The Tinner's, drinking beer out of a bottle like a teenager. She asked his name. 'Mr . . . can't remember,' someone said.

She imagines him shaving in the morning in pyjama bottoms, peering into a speckled mirror that spots his face. He has a mouth that might have turned up once, now it is pinched. His hair is faded, was reddish. Thinning. His eyebrows are a straggle of too-long hairs. He looks wild, energetic. But that may be just illusion.

Now Dodie's thinking too. She's thinking she's never met anyone like this. He stands there in the Stores at different times, day after day, where she can see him, but she's sure he hasn't stood there deliberately. By the bread one day, the tinned food, the next. He sat on the floor once with his head in hands. He is so deep, she thinks. So lost in thought. He was thinking about bread that first time. *Bread.* What about bread? A fundamental of life? Biblical? What, Mother's Pride? Then *tinned food*? Thinking about tinned food? Time, that must be it, with tinned food. Preserving time. Keeping things unspoiled, but in the dark where you can't see them, and they can't see you. Baked beans, own brand cheaper than Heinz. Tomatoes, dented tins cut price. It must all mean something.

Dodie thinks this must have been coming for a long time. She hasn't exactly been waiting for it, more it has been waiting to happen. She knows she's clever, because they told her, years ago at school, she won prizes. Books, with stickers in. Bookmarks. A painted plate.

The Philosopher has been coming for a long, long time. It's been in her horoscope. Over and over she's read it: *Virgo: With the moon in Mercury, you're going through a difficult time in your love life. But your time will come. Your even temperament will please someone who needs you.*

Dodie the *Virgo*. She knows, because she's read it so many times: *Only 5% of females are still virgins at the age of forty-five.*

She's forty-five before Christmas.

≈

Today The Philosopher stands by the washing powders, fabric conditioner and Fairy Liquid. It's nearly closing time, and Dodie needs to mark some unsold goods with today's sell-by date at half price. She needs to walk past him to collect two Mother's Prides and some malt loaf, some wedges of 'Farmer's Own Choice' cheese and a four pack of cherry yogurt. He says nothing as she passes him. But when she comes back, he's blocking the aisle.

'Excuse me,' she says.

He says nothing but moves back. Then, when Dodie is touching him with her arms, holding the goods close to her breasts, because he has not moved quite far enough, he says, his voice so close to her ear that she jumps,

'I'm still thinking.'

'What about?'

'Guess.'

Dodie looks round, sees a Fairy Liquid bottle. 'Recycling?' she says, 'Reincarnation?'

The Philosopher smiles, kind of. 'How clever,' he says. 'We are on the same wavelength.'

'Are we?' says Dodie, nonplussed, putting half-price stickers on the malt loaf. The Philosopher puts a hand on the loaf, catching two of her fingers under his. She jumps again. His breath smells sweet-heavy.

'I'll have this,' he says. 'And that,' he nods his head at the bread and cheese, 'when you've finished.' He waits.

Dodie adds the prices up wrong. Blushes.

'When you've finished . . .' he repeats.

'Sorry.'

'. . . we could talk about thinking. At the pub.'

'Sorry?'

'Well?'

She was right. It was coming. He was always coming, and she should have been ready. He'd seen something in her that she hasn't met herself yet, and she didn't *see* it. . . . *your time will come. Your even temperament* . . .

'Yes please.' Dodie says. And knowing she smells of onions, 'Half an hour?'

And Dodie starts to make herself ready. Not just herself, although this is unconscious. Her room is as tired as she is. The bed slumps; what was bright pink candlewick is faded, uneven, the fringe pulled, trailing on the rug. There is a framed print above the bed of the sea crashing against rocks; someone, a long time back, pencilled a boat in one corner. She tried to rub it out but it's still there, a stick man waving through the ocean at her. Dodie takes down the unlined cotton curtains and takes off the bedspread, bundles them together and puts them in the downstairs washing machine. That makes her feel better.

Later, in The Tinners, they sit together in Dodie's corner, on sagging burgundy plush cushions. He has bought her a cider, he drinks beer from the bottle. They talk. Dodie is half listening, looking at the scratches through the varnish on the table ... the number four among the scratches.

Bill calls over. 'Dodie? You OK, love?'

The Philosopher answers, before she does, 'She's fine.' Dodie just looks up and smiles.

'Look,' Dodie says, tracing the scratches with her finger. 'Number four.'

'It will mean something,' he says 'You wait.'

And Dodie waits, breathlessly, drinking in instances of the number four the next day. Four silver cars in a row outside the General Stores. Four stamps on a letter from New Zealand awaiting collection under the counter of the post office shelf. Four brown moles on her left thigh. Four packets of condoms sold to the driver of the paper van.

She's picking up some apples that have fallen onto the floor. A voice close to her ear, a hand on her shoulder. 'So, what did the number mean?' Dodie drops the apples. Four of them.

'I don't know ...' she breathes.

'Yes you do,' he says. 'You have the gift.'

Dodie straightens up, the apples in her hands. 'Have I?' she says, eyes bright.

And so it goes on. Dodie's curtains are rehung. She cleans her room over and over, getting down on her knees to wipe the skirting board with a blue cloth. She buys herself some hair colour, first time ever. *Chestnut lights*, it says, and it splashes in the sink, works its way into the cracks round the plughole. Leaves her hairline looking dark, dark. She tries the lipsticks, buys a chalky pink one, *Moonflower*.

Bill at the pub keeps asking if she's OK. She smiles every time.

Four days. They've been 'going out' for four days, and people are smiling at Dodie, not at The Philosopher, and she thinks they mind about something. Maybe they are jealous because not everyone can think so deeply. Today, today, today and today. Four of them. He's so clever. He thinks about hedges, drainage ditches, yellow diggers, dead crows, sheep's wool, and seaweed. He says there is so much to think about in this life.

Dodie breathes faster. She searches for things, finds them, throws things out for him to think about.

'What about beer mats? Darts? Chipped pint mugs? Alcopops? Boiled eggs? Coffee?'

The Philosopher smiles and pats her hand. She doesn't jump any more. 'Some things are deeper than others,' he says. 'I'll teach you.'

And she listens looking through him, her lower *Moonflower* lip hanging loose as he thinks in streams about newspapers, printing ink and trees, the 'circle' as he calls it of capitalism (where, he says, lots of people work in a circle, or a spiral, doing things made necessary by the 'work' done by the person before, but take them all out, and the world wouldn't suffer). Sometimes he bangs the table with his fist and her cider jumps and Bill looks over and raises an eyebrow.

∿

It's late on the fourth day. She's going for a walk with The Philosopher today. He's coming for her soon, half an hour after closing time he said, seven thirty they close. Eight he'll come.

They'll walk down the lane towards the beach, and they will think as they go about bungalows, lamp posts, telegraph poles maybe. *Communication.* That's it. Tarmac, double yellow lines and crows flying high up above the bent fir trees. Wind. She'll ask him what wind is, because you can feel it, but can't see it, and that must be like God. Or is it the world turning faster and faster and faster so in the end everyone will fall over? She laughs at the thought and feels the power of it.

Dodie remakes her bed and buys herself some freesias from the bucket outside the door of the Stores. Yellow like slab cheddar. And lilac. She cuts the stems, puts them in a handle-less mug painted with a boat flying the Cornish flag, and the freesias splay out on the chest of drawers, hanging in her room like aliens. She showers, using a new shower gel the girl surfers buy, which smells of lemons and limes. She puts on a flowered skirt she hasn't worn for years, a white blouse. *Moonflower.*

The lane is quiet. They pass the bungalows, and just as she knew they would they think about bungalows. About old people, zimmer frames and holiday-makers, buckets of dead whelks. They pass the telegraph poles, wires, and she was right, they think about the buzz of conversation, and she brings in God then, about how God can differentiate between prayers and ordinary conversation. About whether whispering is a better way to communicate than shouting, about letters from new Zealand that no one picks up, and she's sure it's a woman's writing.

They pass the barley field and think about the razored stalks, about harvest mice displaced, and she feels the sadness of it.

They walk on to the beach, the sea pounding to their left, the dunes on their right. They pass three herring gulls tearing at a dead catfish, and they think about predation, food chains, starving and feasting. The beach is empty, and it's getting cold. The sun is still up there, just.

The Philosopher has been holding her hand. His grip tightens a little and she starts to think about her room, the curtains, how the sun will come through the curtains early in the morning, the freesias. The stick man in his boat. She wants to tell The Philosopher about the stick man, because it must mean something, and he says, 'Let's sit down here,' pulling her towards the dunes. But Dodie doesn't want to go there. She wants to go back to her room, because her horoscope did say, . . . *your time will come. Your even temperament will please someone who needs you.*

But he doesn't listen. He's not saying what he's thinking any more, and their footsteps, which had left regular tracks in the damp sand, flat flat sand right to where the waves are beating, become crossed, muddled, fast.

Dodie stumbles on the dry sand of the dunes as he pulls her up the side. 'Why?' she says. 'Why are we going here?' and she says something about freesias and stick men and The Philosopher says nothing, just pulls, pushes, doesn't even look at her face, pulls, pushes, pulls, pushes and hurts her.

∾

He doesn't come in to the General Stores the next day.

At the end of that day, Dodie walks down the lane, waiting for the thoughts to come. She passes the bungalows, and they are just bungalows, their windows blank. The telegraph poles carry wires that hum in the wind. The barley stalks have cut her legs. She walks along the beach, looking to see if the tide has left any footsteps. They are there, somewhere, she thinks, even though their shape has gone.

She sees a young couple walking, the girl's hair blowing over her face like a veil, and she feels the sadness of that.

She waits for them to pass and climbs slowly up the dune, searching. The grasses are still flat, but the breeze has softened the shadows in the sand. The place is healing itself. But there, at the bottom of the hollow, a gull has had a meal, and the sand holds white bone, red bone, skin, and Dodie doesn't want to see it.

She tries to make something out of yesterday's incident that is not hopeless. She won't allow herself to name the act that happened here, and will wonder, if someone takes something you were going to give them anyway, is that stealing? She will think. In time her thoughts will become memories, and she will recall a little kindness where in fact there was little, and some meaning where there was none at all.

THE LYCH-WARMER

NO ONE NOTICED the sand. The church of St Just and St Sebastian had only ever been lit dimly, by the sun filtering through stained glass windows, or by candlelight. No one noticed little Meggie Lightfoot, the church cleaner, bringing in sand in the pockets of her child-sized jumble-sale raincoat with its belt tied in a greasy knot. No one noticed her taking pinches of sand between arthritic finger and thumb, riffling it into dark unsung places; into the footless corners of box pews, into the solemn crevices behind the pulpit steps, into the slump of once-bright pamphlets in the Sunday School corner, and beneath the altar cloth, heaping it quietly against shy and shrouded legs.

And, no one noticed, half way down the church, behind an old oak chest used as a side altar under the window of St Sebastian, that the sand was a little deeper, a little thicker, a little more carefully spread. For little Meggie Lightfoot was waiting for her due: a miracle.

~

Meggie's knobbled hands, her bent neck and spine, every bone in Meggie's body, her slight scaffolding, was crumbling. She had felt her vertebrae rubbing together, every movement like millstones grinding, grinding, grinding her bones into something that trickled to her extremities, pushing to return to the earth, dust to dust.

70

It is important to understand that Meggie was the last of the line. No cousin to intermarry as generations had for so long, providing a constant enzyme to digest Lightfoot life and return it to the earth.

So. Sand?

The church and its graveyard were besieged by dunes which lay between sea and village like a school of mouldering whales. But Meggie found her sand, not between the tangled marram roots anchoring the dunes, nor on the childless beaches with their black mussel-sharp headlands pointing like dead fingers out to sea, but in the churchyard, at a lichen-tumbled grave of one Althea Lightfoot, her ancestor. A grave apart, near the lych-gate.

IN LOVING MEMORY OF ALTHEA LIGHTFOOT, the gravestone still says in its rough touchfinger tongue. LYCH-WARMER, WIDOW OF (here the stone is worn). FELL ASLEEP IN THE LORD 9TH FEBRUARY 1856

Here, in one grave that gave up sand, lies, in one body, Meggie's great-great grandmother and grandmother-in-law, and her great-great aunt and aunt-in-law, a woman somewhere on the complicated degenerating spiral that was Lightfoot blood.

Perhaps it was small blind animals that snouted the sand up from the breathless dark into the light? Perhaps not. Perhaps it is all just a story? But one story that is not a story at all was Meggie's foundation; that of Althea Lightfoot, the village lych-warmer, a story that ran in Meggie's blood as sure and necessary as oxygen.

The story is this; how Althea Lightfoot lost her husband and they not wed more than a few weeks when his fishing boat sank further than the sound of a shepherd's whistle out into the Atlantic. How she was already with child. How his body was found, perfect, on the rocks at Prussia Cove a few days later and he so handsome that the fish had not so much as nibbled at his eyelids. How there was no money for a coffin, and her man's body was left to spend its last night at the lych-gate, wound about in its shroud. How Althea came that night, dew on her shawl like diamonds, and lay with her man under the lych-gate, warming him, he who had lain with the fishes.

How, in the morning, they came and found her wound about with her man in his shroud. How they pulled her, heavy with sleep, from his arms and slid him into the ground.

How, when the next villager died, they came to Althea and asked her not to let the warmth leave his body before the farewell, and how from then on she was the village lych-warmer, spending the last night with the coffined and the uncoffined under the lych-gate in whatever weather came. How, when her daughter was born, she became lych-warmer too, and the two of them could be seen, sometimes heard, singing rhymes to the dead and the undead, the buried and the not yet buried, keeping them warm for that last night above ground while their families sat behind black windows.

How, years later, on a Sunday night when the wind howled fit to claw down Heaven itself, another fishing boat and her crew were lost, together with eight men, their friends, who rowed out over the heaving seas to die with them. How four pilchard fishermen and an apprentice, three tin miners, the ploughman, Lemuel the stonemason, Sebastian the elderly Minister's only son down from Oxford, mute Jacob the giant with the strength of six, and carpenter Harris who made, last, his own coffin, were drowned, as they had lived, together.

How none could be buried until they all were found. How their bodies were brought on another cold night to the church and laid on the flagstones before the altar. How Althea Lightfoot and her daughter lay there with them all and warmed them for the last time.

How the bereaved Minister and his wife, numb with grief, had a new window painted for their church in their son's memory and in his close likeness as St Sebastian pincushioned with arrows. How the church of St Just embraced the dedication of window in name and deed. And how, over time, the story gathered itself together and drew up from a collective and deep tradition the promise of a miracle, as yet undelivered, from St Sebastian in gratitude to the Lightfoot women.

∾

Take then, this lifeblood of Meggie Lightfoot, and add to it one little day in Advent years before the time when sand came into church, a day when sleet was slicing at the stone walls of the village, and when Meggie was to clean the window of St Sebastian, this being its centenary and it being mazed with candle-grime and dust.

Add a vision of Meggie slipping from her high bed in her house overlooking the dunes on the very edge of the village, the Lightfoot house for as long as anyone can remember, the bed in which she was both conceived and born, and her mother before her and her mother before that, back and back and back until darkness falls over memory, or story. Watch her leave the house, pulling the collar of her raincoat round her ears, lifting her sharp face for a second to acknowledge the smell of low-tide seaweed in the sleet. Watch her, back to the wind, knotting her belt, tying her headscarf tight under her chin. See under that raincoat an old oiled-wool fisherman's sweater belonging to her dead father, a blue overall and scuffed brown leather sandals with one buckle hanging by a thread. Put in her hands a basket of cleaning cloths and sponges, and half run with her through the dunes to the lych-gate. Pause with her as she pauses, writing her frozen initials in the sleet on the stone bench then putting her forefinger in her mouth. Push open the church doors with her and enter its heavy penumbral chill. Wait while your eyes take in what light there is and magnify it.

Lay at her feet an old dented metal bucket half full of warm soapy water. Find her a wooden step ladder and lean it against the peeling wall under the saint's window. Steady it on the uneven flagstones with an open hymn book. It does not matter.

And set little Meggie, the virgin, to work.

How does she feel climbing the steps to join St Sebastian when she, grounded, has looked up at him a thousand times? How does she feel not raising her eyes to his body, yet, but taking her cloth and rubbing a low corner of the glass, misting a small circle for a while then taking a second cloth and drying, polishing?

You cannot say. But there, in that first ungrimed circle, see what she sees where she thought to find roughly painted grass, or rocks. Instead, tiny Cornish squill flowers the colour of a pale April morning, kindly speedwell, gentle camomile with leaves as feathery as the summer carpets on the headlands, the scarlet stars of periwinkles, and little chips of sunlight masquerading as bird's foot trefoil, buttercups and celandines. She widens the circle and discovers ragged robin, poppies, daisies, tamarisk and montbretia, daffodils, narcissi, and, round the lower edge of the window, brambles laden with fat black-berries, boughs blue with sloes and bullaces, crab apples. And, among the flowers the bare feet of the saint overgrown with ivy fronds, his skin brown and healthy, the nails square, strong.

She runs her fingers over tufts of brown hair on the big toes. She washes those feet as gently as if she were washing the feet of a dying man, and in the end, it is the hair on the toes, the simplest most human of things, which brings tears.

Do you look away while Meggie cries? Do you pretend inter-est in the rising motes while she wipes her tears on her cleaning cloth and carries on with her work? Are you cold? Sit in Meg-gie's box pew then, and wrap yourself in your coat, conjured for the purpose. Creak the door to, and wait, out of the draught. It is not easy to watch Meggie at her window. It intrudes. But she is so taken up with belonging that she would not mind.

She has washed his feet with her tears. She has cleared the ground on which he stands against his stake, naked save for a soft cloth round his hips. She has moved the step ladder again and again, climbing up and down, replenishing the water in her bucket, dirty for clean. She has cleansed the sky, letting loose gannets, fulmar, a pair of peregrine that tumble out of the enamel blue. She has set free the ocean beyond the painted headland, still now, and she has her head on one side, see? She is listening for guillemots and razorbills, herring gull and eider, and for the pulse of wave against rock.

Against all this solid nature, the flesh of the pinioned saint is as transparent as an egg's membrane under its blanket of wax and dust. As Meggie runs her cloth down his thigh, the sleet beats outside against his muscles, pauses for a second as though testing the temperature, then gives up and slides down the glass. Through his thighs she sees the lych-gate, through his

75

stomach the yew-tree, through his chest the dry stone wall and the arching tamarisk.

She wonders at the arrows embedded in him and at the lack of lifeblood, as though they had hit a body in which the veins were empty. She washes each wound as though she were a nurse, changing the water often, massaging his straining shoulders, knowing his wrists are tied out of sight with a rope smelling of fish, rough, tight with salt.

His face. Imperfect, unshaven, real. Lips tight against the onslaught, a hollow where he bites the inside of his cheek, a bruise purpling one cheekbone. Curls tumbling in the breeze. Unkempt eyebrows and eyes that do not gaze heavenwards in ecstasy, but straight into those of Meggie Lightfoot.

~

Why then, twenty years later, dying, did Meggie bring him sand? She did not believe in much, the Lightfoot faith having diminished with each successive generation, but she knew that somehow, glass was fashioned out of sand. She believed unwaveringly that St Sebastian needed sand and had asked her to bring it to him. She believed this from that quiet place beyond the merely visceral, the place where things simply are, without question. She waited for the miracle that would come.

But stories that are indeed stories, do not finish as those who people them might wish. They finish untidy, open-fingered, clutching at air. Look.

The sand dunes were shifting. The walls of the church were crumbling. There came a time that autumn when cracks started to appear round the window of St Sebastian. There came a day when workmen, repairing the wall, removed the window in its entirety, laying it gently on blankets on the flagstones in front of the altar. They blocked its hole with board. They moved the oak chest in front of the window and found Meggie's sand. Then, thinking it had come through the cracks in the wall, they brushed it away, every last grain.

~

There are accounts of the two days and nights of 26th and 27th November 1982. They tell of high tides and a fast level wind that blew off the sea, strong and persistent. They tell of the wind so full of whipping sand that most people would not leave their houses. This much is fact. They tell of the uprooting of the marram and the slow march of the dunes towards the church, a tumbling and a rolling of minute grains, building up and sliding down until they poured through the lych-gate before breaching the dry stone wall and digesting the tamarisk. They tell how the church doors were not secured, but opened like a gaping mouth when the sand shouldered them wide. This too is fact.

There are accounts of how the villagers dug their way into church two days later, burrowing, working like frantic ants whose nest has been trodden by a giant foot. There are accounts of how the sand had rolled into the church but stopped in front of the altar, on the flagstones where St Sebastian was so carefully laid on his blankets, and how the villagers, frightened that their window would be broken beyond repair, stood round about, caps in hand as though at a funeral.

There are accounts of the finding of Meggie Lightfoot's body under the sand, spread-eagled, face down, on the rough blankets where St Sebastian should have been.

Some say she went to the church to move the window out of the path of the sand, and fell. Some say she found it stolen and was overcome. Some say that, below her body, still warm, they found a different sand. Whiter, purer, with residues of plant ash and traces of enamel pigment. Who is to say that this is not fact?

~

Now, below the dry stone wall near the lych-gate there is another Lightfoot grave, the last. It too gives up sand. Nothing is still; all is flux. Glass, it is said, is merely a state of matter.

THE CAROB TREE

NO. I DON'T *care* what your agenda is. I'm Miguel. I'm telling you about Pepito. I will have to tell you because he can't, not now, and I think he is important, in his way. So just for a few minutes, still the buzzing, OK?

Pepito's island? Oh, it is beautiful. We always knew that. The sea is the blue of Heaven, the blue of the Virgin's robes in the pictures in our church. The old women used to bring flowers, you know? But I'm getting ahead of myself.

Pepito and I, we were born almost together. Our village, San Carlos, a straggle of white walls in a red soil, exactly like seabirds resting on a flat red sea. The biggest bird, the church. Whitewashed, hunchbacked with its chapel to the side. Pepito said it was like a gull with a broken wing, it might try to fly up into the sky and get stuck, flying round in circles and never quite make it to God.

Outside the church is the carob tree.

They said Pepito's mother and mine were friends. I never knew his mother, neither did Pepito. They used to tell the girls in the village, 'Oh, mind you don't do what Juanita did. Mind you don't wait too late for your babies. The body will break. She was three days and nights in labour, and look at poor Pepito— motherless.' But I never thought of him as 'poor Pepito.' To me, he was wonderful. He saw the houses like birds, and he said so. He saw the church like an injured bird, and he said so. Me, I just saw houses. A church. A white church with three arches in front, and two old bells hanging in the arch on the roof.

They said it was because of the three-day labour, but I say he was special.

What do we do? Oh, I farm. I have my wife, my child, my carob trees, lemon trees, peach trees, my fig trees, my olives. A few almond trees, but they are tricky. I have some chickens, I grow corn under the olive trees, but my corn is full to bursting with poppies.

'Kill the poppies,' they say. 'Kill the poppies and sell the corn, or make bread, Miguel.' So do I? Do I do what they say? I do not. I remember Pepito looking at the poppies, blowing the dust off them, telling me how the smallest things are beautiful.

'Hey, look, Miguel,' (I can still hear him), 'Which is more beautiful? The ear of corn or this one petal?' There is no answer, is there?

We were both born when kingdoms and empires were crumbling. That's what they said. When there were a few cars on the island, but none in San Carlos. And, when I took my place at our farm, and let my father rest, Pepito still helped people.

Oh, didn't I say? Pepito helped. He did nothing for himself, helped everyone. When the baker was taking loaves out of the oven, Pepito knew the place to be, and he would wait with a thick cloth to receive the iron trays and sift flour over the loaves. When the old women were doing the washing, Pepito was there to tell them not to worry about lifting heavy wet sheets to the lines. He would do it.

And he was there, sweeping his church. Yes, his.

Look. Here, the soil is red. It is dry, for months at a time there is no rain (I have an artesian well). Red dust blows against the walls of the houses, stains the damp sheets on the lines, blows through the open wooden doors of the church. It covers walls with a fine layer, so fine you think the white is white, until you look properly. The white is red.

Pepito, years ago, when he was small, helped the women to brush the church every day. Gradually, you see, the women left, knowing that they had other things to do, and Pepito would do it, willingly. Smilingly, because that was Pepito.

He would brush the red dust from the floor, take a soft cloth to the Stations of the Cross, wipe down the altar, candles, dark wooden chairs, every day. And when we had a new priest, when the old man had to go, Pepito was offered the room alongside the chapel to live in.

He was so proud. He walked a little straighter. Said, 'Miguel, now I am a man.' I said, 'Yes, you are,' watching him with his broom, pushing the red dust out of the door where the wind caught it, scurried it in circles and sent it straight back again.

The old men talked about a Civil War. They sat with their small glasses of red wine, hunched over cards, spitting in the dust, talking of a Civil War. They said Nationalists were being caught and imprisoned in D'Alt Vila.

'How can a war be civil?' Pepito asked. They laughed.

There was a day when soldiers came. A day when the priest had gone on his black bicycle to the next village to see a dying woman. We do not know, but we think Pepito was brushing the steps, and shaking out the priest's robes that hung behind the door of the vestry. This is when the soldiers came. And Pepito, who had come to think of this broken winged bird, the church, as his, *his* church, he had put on the priest's garment.

Oh Pepito, my friend.

The soldiers came to the church with their guns. Pepito stood in the doorway, his arms akimbo, and said, 'We will have no guns in the house of the Lord.' He stood in his priestly robes and shunned the soldiers.

One soldier, the chief, maybe, (or maybe not, perhaps the second chief who needed strength), said, 'We are searching for Nationalists. We will search your church.' He went to push past Pepito, who stood his ground, arms outstretched. This is what the women said.

The soldier said he was entering. Pepito said, 'No. Not into my church.'

And oh, Pepito. The priest had hidden Nationalist supporters upstairs, hadn't he? He never said. He just locked the door and told them to be quiet so you never knew.

There is still a tree outside the church, Pepito. A carob tree. You never liked them as a boy. Said the black pods reminded you of dead fingers, do you remember? Said the leaves were too dark.

They chose a young soldier, and they said, 'Hang the priest. Hang him here in the square, from this tree.'

How, Pepito? How did you not say you were not the priest? How did you not show them your brush and your cloths? Your room with its cross on the wall?

The women said the young soldier was flummoxed. He did not know what to do. They, the others, fetched him a rope from the stable, and a chair from the church, an old dark wood chair that you had dusted so often. The women said you stood on it and smiled. They said the young soldier trembled and blanched, that you looked up into the carob tree and smiled. They said you looked at the branches and said, 'The carob tree is not ugly. I thought it was, but it is beautiful. Its leaves are like the hands of children offering butterflies to the sky.'

The young soldier watched his comrades walking into the church, the houses, and he was alone, and he said to you Pepito, 'Please, forgive me. I have heard, if I hang on your legs, at least it will be quick.'

One of the women, Pepito, she said she was so full of tears she could not see. She said she wanted to cry out but couldn't for fear, for fear the soldiers would kill her sons. But, she said, as the soldier pulled the chair away, as he hung fast to your legs, tugging your body down against the noose so your neck might break, she thought she saw you raise your hand in blessing.

Yellow Birds, Beaks Open

I'M JOE. BILLY, he was my mate. Always looked wise but hurting like Jesus being nailed to the cross.

Billy said he had headstones. I said what did he mean, like lice? Like things sticking out between his hair, in the parting or what? Billy said no, sometimes when he shook his head it was full of pebbles, he could feel them slapping against each other tink-clinking in his skull. I said if they make sounds like that they must be dead small stones, nothing to worry about, what's the bother 'cos you've got no brain anyway. Billy laughed.

'Nah, they's great big rocks,' he said, 'that sort, listen.' He shook his head like there was a drum beat going on, his hair flew in spikes. 'Can you hear them?' He shook and shook his head. I couldn't hear them.

'Well, that's your problem,' he said.

When he dropped Es, then he heard them. No need for drums, electronic beats, any beats. Thud thud thud. He just pumped his head up down all night in the club, could out-dance us all.

I thought they were good things, Billy's stones. He said no. He said they made his head hurt like it was in a vice. They were trying to push out of his eye sockets, out of his mouth. He felt sick. Sometimes he *was* sick, and it didn't make any difference. No stones came up; just thin yellow liquid.

'Jeez,' I said. 'Bill, got no pride haveya?'

He said 'Pride? What's that?'

Tried to get me to drop Es but I never did. They all said I was a wimp. But I like watching my back, know what I mean? Clubbing's OK, if you've got the money.

I didn't see him for a bit. Heard it wasn't Es any more. Right tough stuff now. I went to see him at his old place, they said he'd moved on, gave me some girl's address.

He was there. Said he'd *had* a job. Said he'd lost the job but still got the money. Still got the headstones. His eyes were red, he shook his head up down up down, "See? You can hear them now, can'tcha?'

Course, I still couldn't. Said so too, then he got down. Kept shaking his head, said could I give him twenty. No mention of any of the rest I'd given him ages back.

I gave him thirty because I had it. He pulled on a jacket, went out without looking round.

I saw Billy after that, now and again. Precinct, arcade. He got thinner, didn't look too bad. Didn't have a job, always trying for money. His girl Mellie was sweet, didn't say much, just clung onto him. Tiny, bony, short black hair, eyes blue like ice. At least I thought she was sweet at the time, now I think poison ivy.

He used didn't he? She used; where they got the cash from is a mystery. I wondered if I ought to tell someone, got these leaflets, took them round to their place, they were asleep on the floor.

She disappeared overnight. Billy didn't know where she'd gone, but I heard she'd found a bloke who was giving her stuff while she worked. You know. So she never went back. I stayed now and again when he got down.

I watched him one time shooting up, he smiled at me, Jesus about to get nailed to the cross, said 'It ain't that bad.' Then his eyes misted and he went.

But it was bad. I stayed, he woke, half. Those were no good dreams he was having. Screaming for his Mum, clutching at my hand like it was a lifeline, crying real tears. I wanted to leave, couldn't. He'd go quiet, I'd think he was asleep. Then he'd wake, surface, whatever, roll his eyes, cry for his Mum.

Like a small kid was in his skull trying to get out, crying. Like this kid was in there being battered by the stones in his head, falling and bashing in a giant tumble dryer smashing this little kid, his bones breaking slowly over and over.

Sometimes, even though you care there's nothing you can do. It's like being down a pitch dark pit with the air sucked out and yellow birds, beaks open at the bottom of cages.

I left him in the morning. I thought, look Joe, you've got your own life to live. There's a lot to do out there, Billy'll only drag you down. Look at what he's doing already. (I'd jacked in my job three times, given him my money, it wasn't helping him or me. I still feel bad when I look back).

I left him to it.

Then the November I saw him again. Bonfire night. Watching the fires with my OK mates, drinking, laughing, pissing about. Billy was slumped in a doorway when we went to get a kebab. He looked bad. Really bad. Shaking. I bought two kebabs, two of us hoiked him under the arms, took him back to his place. Same place, but stinking. Piss. Shit.

Billy didn't want to eat. He cried, said he needed more. 'What's it about Bill?' I said. 'What's it about?'

'It's about nothing, mate. It's about fucking nothing.' He shook his head. I thought I knew what he was hearing. 'I can't even fucking hear them any more,' he said. He was crying snot into his mouth. 'I liked those stones, they were, like, different, you know?'

He needed. He was my mate, needed something. Am I a friend? I dunno. He got his stuff, and I watched him, like Jesus he was again. This smile, this pale thin smile like he knew everything in the world and it was just too sad to hold it in. Then he lost it, slowly.

Before he went he said quietly, shaking his head, 'Can you hear them now, mate? You must be able to hear them.'

I held his shoulders. Before his eyes shut I told him. I said, 'Billy, I hear them, mate. I do.'

CACTUS MAN

ONE

SOCIAL WORKERS. 'I'M Angela,' she says. Open-toed sandals. Hairy ankles. Small talk in the lift. Graffiti on the mirrors, etched like train windows. Smell of civil service dust and stale cigarettes under a 'No Smoking' sign.

Then her office. How does she breathe? I want to open the window, let in some air. She pulls out a chair and she's sitting opposite. Our knees are nearly touching.

'Now,' she says. 'Yours is an interesting case.'

Her desk is cluttered, haphazard. Unfinished business. This *chlorophytum* is just by her. Grey as the cabinet it's on, lank as a probation officer's dick. She's fingering one leaf, running her nail up and down.

'You shouldn't do that,' I say. 'They don't like it.'

She jumps like the leaf is hot. 'The spider plant? Sorry, I didn't know.'

'You know what they do? They absorb toxins from the atmosphere.'

She looks at the *chlorophytum* like it's just spoken or something. To me it looks like it's soaked up all the grief that's ever been through this room.

'I was saying how unusual your case is.'

'Can't be doing with too much usual.'

88

'Sorry?'

'We feed off being unusual, us lot.'

'Oh, I see.'

This Angela, she leans forward at me like she wants to read my small print. She's got brown eyes. She was probably pretty once. Not that she's old. But she just looks tired. 'I need to know why,' she says. 'Why now?'

I'm looking past her. Cacti on the windowsill. Stunted, pots too small.

'Why not?' I say. 'Are those *mammillaria* yours?'

She smiles. 'The cacti? Yes, sorry. I'm not much good with plants.'

'They'd look healthier if you looked after them,' I say. 'That little round one is from Mexico. *Mammillaria bombycina*.'

'Is it?'

'It should have babies attached to it by now. Round the base. Try putting it in the sun.'

'OK. I will.' she says, then, gently, 'Spike? Why now? You're twenty-two. You've had four years.'

'If you were called Spike you'd want to know your proper name.'

There's not enough room here for my legs. My knees are starting to ache. I rub them. My hands brush her skirt.

'I'm getting married,' I tell her. 'April. I need a proper name for chapel.'

She turns sideways and crosses her legs. Her foot is pulsing gently up and down. 'That's lovely. Date?'

'The something. Elaine would kill me if she knew I'd forgotten.'

'Elaine?' She's taking notes, using a file to lean on.

'Yes,' I say. 'I've known her since—'

'Since?'

'Since my third mam, I think. The nice one, who died. Mam Thomas from Gwilym Terrace. Elaine lived in Gwilym Terrace. We used to play up the tip. We called it 'catching ponies'. Only we never did. They were way too fast.'

I see Elaine, late, running in to my eighth birthday tea, black with coal dust, hair in her eyes, laughing, her party frock all muddy. She's panting. 'Spike, come and see, fast. There's two foals down by the railway line!' That's it. We're kicking away our chairs, Mam Thomas is shouting at me to take my coat, I've grabbed a handful of cakes, and we're scorching down to the railway, me scattering crumbs, the two of us laughing like banshees.

'But you did have a name before?'

I hardly hear her.

The ponies, on the patch of wasteland by the tracks. Two foals, still trying to balance, steam in their nostrils. The mother, unmoving, her neck at an odd angle. It's so real, I can't swallow.

Her fingers touch my arm. 'Spike? You had a name before?'

I need air. 'Yes. Ages back, I was called Algernon.' I breathe deeply. 'I was called Algernon for years until I became Spike.'

'Go on,' she says.

'This teacher. Miss Edwards. She had all these cacti on the windowsill in her classroom. She got sick. I took them home to look after them for her, but she never came back. I started collecting them then. It was a joke, Spike. But it stuck.'

'I like it,' Angela says. 'It suits you.'

I look at her. I go to get up and our knees touch. She's blushing. We both move our hands at the same time. They brush, then fly apart like sparks.

'Sorry.' I say. I go to the window. I stand, look out over the valley, at the black line of the hills against a sky grey as a dove's belly. The light is fading.

'I remember Mam Thomas telling me the coal tips used to glow when the sun hit them. The bits of coal were so small no one could pick them up. They used to catch the light like they were diamonds.' I run my fingers over the sill. 'Now there are whinberries. Black and blue. If you know where to go.'

'You can see my old school from here,' I hear Angela say. Close. 'And the park. It's nice.'

She must have got up. I can feel her standing behind me. She smells of ice cream. 'A nice view. I watch the rugby sometimes. Or the cricket in summer. I prefer the cricket, really. It's more peaceful.'

'Oh, you must have seen me, then,' I say. 'Fly half in winter, slow left hand spin in summer.' Silly, but I almost expect her hand on my shoulder. It doesn't come. I try to sense her there, but she's sat down again. I turn round.

Suddenly, she's busy. Pulls open a drawer, pushes it back. A metallic snap. She says, 'I don't understand, Spike. What's wrong with being Algernon for chapel, just for one day?' She reminds me of a teacher now.

'I can't be Algernon. Everything's ever gone wrong, it's always Algernon.'

I look back to the hill opposite. Charcoal fading into a charcoal sky. 'My record is under Algernon, isn't it?'

'Well, yes,' and she's flipping a file open. 'Look,' she says, and her eyes are laughing as though she thinks smiling's out. 'There's the shoplifting.'

She's holding a small piece of flimsy paper. Pale blue.

'Shoplifting?' I say. 'I reckon the shop should have been done for cruelty. They'd got this plant, *Saintpaulia* — fallen out of its pot on the floor. Bright blue flowers, black soil everywhere. I took it for Mam Thomas after she got sick and I'd been moved. I took it to take to her in hospital. But I got caught.'

She takes out another sheet, pale green this time. 'What's that?' I say.

She is smiling now. 'Natalie Cummings' she says.

'Oh Christ, Nightly Cummings. 'Twice Nightly'. We had bets who would do it with her first, because she did it with everyone in the end. I won. Then she tried to say I forced her because I wouldn't do it with her a second time, said I'd, you know, but I hadn't.'

'I know. It's all here.'

'So, you can see what I mean. Algernon's not me any more. Never was.' I turn to the cacti. 'Know what this one's called?'

Angela shakes her head.

'It's another *Mammillaria*. *Mammillaria zephyranthroides*. Only this one's different. It doesn't grow babies. 'Stays solitary' — that's what the books say.'

She doesn't say anything.

'But this name business,' I say. 'Elaine says my mam must have called me something. That's why I'm here. Please. For my name.'

She indicates for me to sit back down.

'Know why its called *Mammillaria*? 'I don't wait for an answer. 'They're like nipples.'

Angela peers over. Her eyes are heavy again. Exhausted.

'Where's the toilet?' I ask.

When I come back there's this buff folder on her lap. Brand new. She puts one hand on the cover, as though the words inside will come right through to her fingers. There are scratches on the back of her hand.

She's moved the chairs a bit, because our knees don't touch now.

'So what's my name then?' I ask.

'It's not as simple as that,' she says.

I wait.

'How do you know all this stuff about plants?' she says. Then she runs her fingers through her hair, as though it used to stay there. It flops back.

I shrug. 'I read it.'

'Tell me, Spike . . . .' she says. Her nose is red round the nostrils. She pauses. Her foot is pulsing up and down again, one-two, one-two. 'Tell me what you know about your birth circumstances.'

I get up. Back to the window. It's shit out there. I strain to see the hill.

'It's all there, isn't it?' I say. 'In the file, I mean. Some girl in Cardiff.' I think I can make the hill out, but the colours merge. They flow, and I can't separate them. 'My dad must have been a rugby player. Got it all over me, don't you think?'

She doesn't answer. I look back at her but she is looking so hard at the file, like her eyes are glass in the sun and it'll burn to ash.

I sit again, and she says: 'Were you told that?'

'No. I just — I just think she was little, like Elaine, but like me, too, a bit chippy. I must be a bit like her, mustn't I? Probably had a giggle like Elaine's, one that makes you want to laugh too. Eyes that sort of look up at you.' I stop for a second. 'But I suppose that's just me, isn't it?'

'I think so,' she says. 'But everyone needs to have a picture in their heads, don't they?'

I'm thinking. Yes we do. Pictures. That's all we have. Not real ones. Just pictures in our heads. 'Elaine says I could find out. Find out who she is. My mam.'

It's spilling out now. I reach up for the *chlorophytum*. Dusty leaves. I start to stroke it gently, leaf by leaf.

'Elaine says we could ask her to the wedding. It'll be so good for her to see I'm OK?' I laugh. 'Elaine wants to show me off a bit.'

Angela's smiling again. 'Tell me what Elaine would say.'

'Oh, she'd say things like 'Spike has a proper job now. Apprentice down the garage with Mr Evans. Doing well.' And I think my mam would be proud if she knew I had a job. I'd tell her that I am learning all sorts of things with Mr Evans. He says I'm going to be really good.'

I'm following the shape of one grey leaf with my finger. It was greener once, but it's tired, like Angela. Sunk into itself.

'Mam might tell me I've got brothers. That'd be great.' This time I see us, me, a Jimmy, a Craig, arms round, walking away to the pub, heads down, talking, going to the match.

I look up smiling at Angela, but she's watching me and she's not smiling. I don't say anything.

'Spike . . .' she says.

'I'm wrong, aren't I?' I say. 'Why didn't you stop me? She's nothing like that, is she?'

Angela's hands are palm up. Like she's praying, but not in my country. They are very pale, the palms. The fingers are long, narrow.

'So she was a fat old biddy with warts, was she? It was in the dark, down some stinking alley for a fiver?'

Angela shifts in her seat.

The leaf I'm holding is thin. Like its job is over. Needs water. 'I need to know,' I say. 'I need to know what she called me.'

Angela leans forward again. Her hair is dyed. It's not really that colour. It's grey and old. 'I'm afraid you were not named at birth, Spike.'

'You should give that water.' I say. Then she's talking fast and I'm looking at the wall.

'There's no name here. As I said, most unusual.' She stops, puts both hands on the file flat.

I shift in my seat. The leaf breaks away in my fingers. I tear little pieces off it, onto the carpet.

'It happens,' Angela says, then her voice goes so low I'm leaning forward to catch it. 'I'd leave it now. Go to Elaine. Get married. Just do it.'

I screw up the leaf and drop it.

'What are you saying?' I haven't heard my voice like this before. '*Leave it?* That's me — my fucking *life* — in that folder.'

Angela looks hurt and glances at the door. We both go quiet. There's a hush like a funeral. When I speak again, quieter, I'm shaking my head slowly.

'That's *my* story.' I say. 'Not someone else's. My file. My right, isn't it?'

She looks at my hands. They're shaking and I hadn't noticed. I make fists.

She waits. I count to five in my head.

And then she says, quietly: 'You have a right. No question.' She's leaning forward again, and she's circled my two fists with her hands. They're cold.

95

'You don't need to do this.' she says.
I just look at her.

Spider plants. Why do we call them that? Most people don't even like the bloody things. In the wild, they have to be in the warm, where the sun filters through the trees, and you can just hear the sea.

Angela's voice, soft, 'Most birth mothers give baby a name, even though they know it will be changed. A parting gift. I have seen a few cases like this, normally in specific circumstances.' Her voice tails off. There's a hole in the air waiting for my words to fill it.

'What circumstances?' Now I am thinking what's Angela holding back? It's like a film in my head, going so fast, hard to keep up with it. First there's me getting born. My real mam dies. A pretty pale face on a hospital pillow. Then a big mix-up at the hospital. A kidnap. Faster and faster it goes. Night time on the ward, there's a man, hunched over, a white bundle under his coat. No alarm.

But I can't stop Angela's voice. 'Two possible scenarios you must be aware of are incest and rape.' She says. Her voice doesn't change. She rattles out incest and rape as though she's saying Welsh cakes and tea.

I get back up and go to the window again. It's darker, dust grey.

'Over there.' I say. 'The old railway tunnel to Tredegar. That's where I went with Natalie.'

'Can I get you a glass of water?' she says.

'No thanks, not for me, but the plants could do with some.'

She eases out of the office, comes back with a jug. She waters the plants, smiles at me.

I breathe in. I rest a finger on the longest spine of one of the cacti, and press down. I feel the skin begin to give.

'OK. Tell me then.'

And then she says, very, very slowly, 'Spike, I'm so sorry. Your mother was attacked. On the way home from work. She . . . '

'Why don't you just say it?'

'Raped. Your mother was raped.'

The cactus spine breaks through the skin. It must be near the bone, but I'm holding my finger steady as a rock.

~

I don't remember what she says after that. I've tried but it won't come. I think I sit with her for ages, and we don't say much at all.

Except I tell her how to look after her cacti properly. They're special. Just need a bit more care and they'll be fine. Probably better at home, sunny.

A while later, I get up to go. When she takes her hand off my file to say goodbye, she leaves four dark fingerprints.

I leave her office holding the *chlorophytum*. She walks with me to the lift. I turn to say thanks, and she kisses me. A dry whisper-kiss that just misses my mouth.

'It's OK,' I say. 'At least I know what my name is.'

She smiles.

I try to smile back. 'I'll stay with Spike.'

She touches my shoulder and I step into the lift.

TWO

I'm walking away towards the High Street in the damp. It's been drizzling, but it's stopped. The street lights are on. The road shines, orange coal.

I turn and look back at the office block. Lights in reception, a couple of higher windows. I can't see Angela's room, but I can see her in my head, drawing a line under, tidying me away, back into the drawer. I need a drink.

I'm holding the *chlorophytum.* This damp air's good for it. I brush at the leaves to get the air under them, then hold it, almost like a baby. I'm not meeting Elaine until seven.

When I walk in The Crown, a few faces look up. It's smoky, warm. I go to the bar for one, just to settle things. I put the *chlorophytum* down.

The barmaid, smudged eyes, 'One for your friend?' she says, looking at the plant. She leans on the bar and smiles. Christ.

A few pints later I hear my voice, 'Mine shafts.'

She's drinking with me, 'What?'

'We dig our shafts, they go parallel, straight down.' My laugh is too loud. 'This guy's was OK. Started off rubbish, but, hey, now it's fine.' She's looking into my eyes. I look away, at the bottles behind her.

'Sometimes, these shafts, they get too close to each other. Doesn't matter how far down you are, how much you think it's just you, your shaft, the walls between can give. Wham! your life is mixed with someone else's. The walls are gone, the earth falls in, and what was yours gets mixed up with what was theirs.'

She's stroking the back of my hand with her finger. I look down, then look at her face. She's smiling, but only with her mouth.

'Of course it does.' she says.

I pull my hand away. I look at the clock. It's gone seven.

'I've got to go,' I say

When I get outside, the air hits me like a fist. I run to The Crawshay, I don't stop. I just run to Elaine.

It's freezing, but she's waiting outside, sitting on a low brick wall, chewing a strand of her hair. She sees me coming and gets up, a smile so wide. She runs towards me, her heels clicking on the pavement.

Her hug nearly knocks me off my feet. Her curls have tightened in the damp. She's put eye shadow on.

'What's that?' she says, looking at the *chlorophytum*, her hands under my jacket. I don't know why I don't answer.

She digs her chin into my chest and looks up into my face. I can feel her body through her coat. 'You've been drinking,' she says.

'Just the one,' I say. I put my arm round her and we go inside.

'So who am I marrying then?' she says when we sit down.

'Me,' I say, thinking, me, the bloke you were with this afternoon.

'Ah, go on, daft thing. What was the social worker like? What did she tell you? Can we ask your mam to the wedding?'

'Look,' I say. 'It's not as easy as that.' I push my fingers into the hard earth round the *chlorophytum*, breaking it up.

She's looking at me, waiting, 'What?'

'I wasn't called anything,' I say. 'Nothing at all.'

I'm expecting a pause, Elaine to go quiet. But it's only a second. 'So she didn't call you anything? That's funny.'

'No.'

'Well, *I* still love you,' she says. Then she says it again as if it will make it twice as real. '*I love you.*'

'I need another pint,' I tell her.

Later, we're walking home. We've got past the shops, the cinema. We cross the playing fields and we're by where the Tredegar line was, by the tunnel.

It's dark down there. It's cold. Elaine pulls me in for a kiss, leaning close against the wall. My shoes squeak on cinders as I bend to her mouth. She's warm, soft. Her tongue baits mine. She catches my lip between her teeth, nips at it, giggling. I can taste her, smell lemonade. I'm breathing faster.

'Look it's not—'I get out, because it's not fair. Elaine wants to wait for the wedding. This sort of thing winds me up.

But her hands are everywhere. Her fingers are playing me, stroking me. She moves her hips slowly against me.

'Fair,' I say, and then there's something. Black flashes, like someone has pushed between us. I drop the *chlorophytum* and now it's like there's someone else here, not me. This other person's here, his tongue in Elaine's ear, his hands on her, rougher than before. He's rubbing Elaine's breasts with one hand, his other hand moving downwards. She's making small muffled noises like a cat in a sack.

She twists her head away, says, 'Spike, no.' But she doesn't mean it. I know she doesn't. We're getting married, and it was her, wasn't it? She was all over me. She got me like this. I'm kissing her so hard, lifting her up, my hand under her skirt, pulling.

'No, please,' Elaine says again.

It'll be so easy, just there, so easy, so easy. Nothing would be said.

'Please, Spike, please. I want to wait.'

But I don't.

I am lifting her up. We can do it here.

Then I hear him, he's grunting uh, uh, uh, but it's not him, it's me, and the small noise, the little whimpers, they're Elaine, they're Elaine, and she is trusting me to stop, she always trusted me.

And I stop.

I don't know how long I just hold her, but I just hold her. There's a dim light from the footpath and I can just see the *chlorophytum* and the broken pot on the floor. We are together, and now I can smell the damp and the piss of the tunnel and I'm so, so sorry.

We've been crying, both of us, quietly, calming down, but it's then that Elaine says she wants to do it. We can do it now, here in the tunnel, she says.

My foot is touching the *chlorophytum's* broken pot.

'No way,' I say. I manage a little chuckle as I call her a hussy, kiss the top of her head. Then I ask her, 'Say what we always said.'

'We were going to make it special?'

'Yes,' I say and I feel her pull into me tighter than ever. I just hold her as tight as I can.

I can still hear my heart thudding in my ears. Like a clock, ticking.

We pick up the spider plant, take it home.

The Kettle On The Boat

IT IS MORNING. Papa is loading some bags onto our little boat. I ask him where we are going. He says we are going to the other side of the lake.

'Why are we going to the other side of the lake, Papa?' I ask again. Papa doesn't answer me.

'Why are we going, Papa?'

'Little girls ask too many questions,' he says.

Mama is taking down the curtains. There are two cracks in the window. I ask again. 'Mama? Why are we going to the other side of the lake?'

Mama hides her face in the curtains.

Something inside me knows something.

～

I am Qissúnguaq. It is an Inuit name. It means 'little piece of wood'. I am six years old. I live with my Papa, my Mama and my baby sister. On one side of our house is the sea, on the other side is the lake. This lake is so big I cannot see across. In winter the water in the lake freezes as thick as thick. Then the sea freezes. Some men cut blocks of ice and make icehouses.

Once, they cut a block with a fish inside it. The fish looked at me with big eyes. Its mouth was open.

Papa traps animals, shoots them and skins them. In winter the snow is red with blood. In summer he goes out in his boat and catches fish. He guts the fish black red and the birds scream. He hangs the empty fish on wooden gallows in front of our house. They hang there for two weeks. I like to go and visit them, watch their eyes shrivel up, dry and fall out. I keep the birds away.

When the eyes fall out the fish are ready. Mama cuts them down, dries them and packs them in salt, so we have fish to eat when the ice comes back. For a long time there have not been enough fish.

Once, Papa went out to help catch pilot whales. The whales were smooth, shiny and black. They made the water boil with froth. Papa trapped the whales and the water in the bay was as red as the snow. I remember it. There are no whales in the bay now.

Sometimes Papa shoots big geese with his gun. I pull off their feathers and the down flies round the kitchen and tickles my nose, then Mama cooks some meat, dries some on the gallows. The geese have not arrived this year. Papa waited and waited. He had his gun ready behind the door. Now it is too late. They will not come now.

Sometimes there is not enough soup to fill the pan on the stove.

～

I am on our small boat with Papa, Mama and my baby sister. They don't often take little girls out in boats. It is cold, I am bundled up. My cheeks are frozen. The motor is going put-put-put.

103

There is a kettle on the boat. It is our kettle from home, the one that goes 'hushhhh' when it boils. It is balanced on a cardboard box. I wonder if it has water in. Mama is rubbing her fur boot softly up and down the kettle.

I am glad it is on our boat. That kettle is magic. It fills the room with a big cloud, a warm cloud, and the window gets covered in giant's breath. Mama wipes the glass with her fingers and shows me how to make shapes. When Papa comes back from emptying his traps, the cloud escapes and goes outside. It looks like fingers in the air. They mix with his breath then disappear.

Papa is sitting beside me, one hand on the tiller, the other holding my sleeve very tight. I will not fall in, there are not many waves. It is hard to see my Mama's face because she has a hood up. She is opposite me, turned sideways so she is facing Papa, not facing me. She has the kettle near her legs, and my baby sister is on her back in a caribou papoose. I can just see my sister's head. Her eyes are black beads. Black holes in a hood.

It is a long time since I've been out in the boat. It lives in a tin shed next to our house, even in the summer it lives in the tin shed. Papa pulls it up on wooden poles on the ground for it to roll better. I help him rub the weed off it. The weed is green, and the boat is red.

We are going somewhere. It is a special day. This should be fun, but it does not feel like fun in my belly. I want to ask Mama now where we are going. But Papa is cross, so I don't. Mama is busy with my sister, busy keeping the bags and boxes straight against the rocking of the boat. The curtains are in a bag.

The boat rocks on the lake and I hold on. Papa's hand is tight on my sleeve. He lights a cigarette, a dry old cigarette from a tin under the table. Because it is cold, I can make smoke in the air too, and I blow a white cloud when Papa does. I hope it will make him smile. I have not seen him with a cigarette before. Not in his own mouth. I saw a cigarette when they gave one to the man from over the lake.

We do not have much to give to visitors. We do not often have visitors. We are just me, my Papa, Mama and my sister, some fish in salt and some meat. That's all there is.

The kettle boiled for the visitors. The man and woman from over the lake. The man with the cigarette and the woman with a shawl tied under her chin and no smile. She held my arm and felt it. She said I was strong. When the kettle boiled I could not see them for the cloud.

Mama has a big belly under her coat. She says it is a stone in her belly. When she says that I laugh.

I see something. I look up and see a big bird in the sky. I pull Papa. I say, 'Look Papa! It is a goose!'

It is. It *is* a goose, a big fat goose and it flies round so close I can hear wings pushing the air away. It lands on the lake a little way away from the boat. Mama looks at Papa. He looks at the goose.

I say 'Papa? Shall I get the gun and you can shoot the goose for us?' but Papa does not answer. He is watching the sky, and he is sitting up straight. In a while he sits back, and says, 'There is only one goose.'

I am sleepy with rocking of the boat. I rest against Papa and doze. When I wake up, my Mama has the kettle on her lap. I know there is no water in it then. The stone in her belly is pushing the kettle off her knee, but she is holding it there with a mitten. She is holding it to her with one hand on its handle, the other stroking it round.

Now I can see the shore a long way away, and I can see three houses, they are wood. There are no people.

I look at the shore because Mama is looking at the shore. Then I look back at Mama. She is holding her kettle on her knee, holding it tight with her mittens. She has hunched over it. My sister on her back is wriggling, and Mama shrugs her shoulder to move my sister so she is not bent in the papoose. My Mama is holding the kettle like it might break, holding it gently but steady. She is holding it, hunched over, and her lips are moving.

I cannot hear what she is saying. My ears lean forward to listen but all I hear is the slap slap of the lake against the boat, the put-put of the engine, and the whistle of my Papa's breathing.

Something inside me knows something again.

'Mama? Is the kettle to go away?'

Mama does not answer me. She looks up, a fast look. Even though I am small I can feel this: it is a special day, the kettle has to go away. Mama is sad.

I look back at the shore. I look at the shore and the houses, no bigger than my little fingernail when I hold up my hands and squint through my fingers at the sun. So I do that. I cover my face with my hands and look at the houses through my fingers. They move around, they are brown birds that will fly up into the grey sky, wheel about and scream.

As the houses get bigger they rock up and down like they are boats. There are two people there now. I do not think for me at that moment. I think for Mama.

The boat comes to the jetty, Papa throws a rope to the man. It is the man from across the lake. We go up the ladder. Papa and I, we go up the ladder. There is weed on the lower steps. It slips my feet and he holds my hand. He has a bag round his shoulders. At the top I look back into the boat. I wait for Mama, but she does not come. She is not looking at me. She is holding the kettle, looking back over the water.

There is the woman from across the lake. I look up at Papa. I cannot see him properly even though he is close and I can smell his Papa smell. He gives my hand to the woman. I have mittens on, but her hand is hard, cold. Papa gives the bag to the man.

I say, 'Papa . . . ?'

'These people will look after you,' he says.

I stand and let the woman hold my hand. I watch my Papa going back down the ladder.

Then I see a shape in the sky! Behind Papa there is another goose in the sky and I shout to him.

But it is not a goose. It is only another brown bird.

I think I shout, 'Mama?' Then I know I didn't because no noise came out. I only shouted in my head. Mama heard it though.

Papa is starting the motor, pulling on the string, one, two, three. Our little boat is naughty. It only ever starts after five pulls on the string.

Mama nearly stands up. She holds onto the side of the boat and she has the kettle in her other hand. My baby sister and the stone in Mama's belly are so heavy. They bend her over and I think she will break, I can see her trying to stand up straight. And I hear the motor start to go put-put.

My head says 'Mama?' again, and the boat moves away from the jetty. Mama holds on and lifts her head up. I think she is looking at me but I can't see properly. There is too much water.

Then Mama swings her arm and throws the kettle into the lake. Papa catches hold of her and she sits down again. The boat rocks a little.

The kettle bobs on the lake like a round grey bird with a big long beak. It rocks on the water when the boat begins to go away. I don't watch the boat. I watch the kettle rocking on the waves. The kettle-boat-bird. It is coming closer to me, slowly, and I think if I can hold tight to the ladder and go back down, maybe I can get it.

I hold the woman's hand and wish hard for the kettle to come to me. I wish that the man will help me on the ladder and not let my feet slip on the weed. I wish that I can go somewhere where the kettle will send giant's breath round my head so no one can see me.

But my wishes are heavy wishes. They fill the kettle-boat-bird up too much and it tips forward and drinks the lake through its beak. It sinks.

I watch where the kettle has gone. There is a mark on the water and the brown birds are screaming. I look up and follow the boat. It is very small. It is not going the way we have come, it is going a different way. When I look back to the mark, it has gone. When I look back to the boat, it has gone too.

The brown birds here have big beaks. They are screaming over the water. I know, if Papa makes another gallows, and if they hang fish to dry, these brown birds might steal the fish's eyes.

If I am not there to help, how will Mama know when the fish are ready?

THERE WERE TIGERS

ON THE SUNDAY, after his Nan died, Tom left Dad holding her hand and went down to make a pot of tea. He carried the tray up so slowly it was that heavy. It was only afterwards he saw he'd taken up three cups.

On the Monday, at school, at Weekend News Time, he told them all he'd been to the circus. He stood next to Miss Atkins in front of 2A and said: 'My Weekend News, Monday 24th October. It is a fine day today, and it was like that yesterday when Dad took us to the circus. It was great, because my Nan has been ill, but she was much better, and it was good for us to get out, Dad said. He made it a surprise. He didn't tell us where we were going, and I was excited but Nan, oh she likes to know what's on the boil, she says, so she was a bit . . .

'Anyway. We must have driven for miles and miles. We had to stop for petrol, I remember that, because we bought Rolos for Nan, cigarettes for Dad, and chewing gum for me. Dad said it would be cheaper than getting them at the circus.

'The tent was massive. Absolutely massive. I think it must have been white once, but it had gone a sort of dirty white, like gym shoes. And the people, there were so many people, it was scary. But Dad kept hold, with me one side and Nan the other. Pushing through. You could smell the people. A leathery smell, and the animals. Petrol too. When we paid, this woman with the blackest hair I've seen and eyes that watched over our heads said 'No discounts.' That meant, Dad said, that even though I was young and Nan was old, we had to pay the same as him.'

'Thank you, Tom,' said Miss Atkins, but Tom hadn't finished.

'There were tigers.' said Tom. 'Right in front of us. Huge and bright, with eyes that flashed, they were that mean. They stood on tubs and tossed their heads, and the man with the whip only had to use it the once. There were clowns. But I've never really liked clowns. I put my head against Nan's shoulder, and she said not to worry, she didn't really like them either so we could not like them together.

'But the best bit of all was the trapeze. High, high up against the roof, on silver wires. There were two trapezes, one each side of this huge drop, and no safety net. So high it made your neck hurt to look up. And four acrobats in pink and gold tights and ballet shoes, but muscley arms so I knew they were strong. And they swung backwards and forwards, and flew and caught each other, and hung by the knees, then one dropped and we all thought he was going to crash but he bounced back on a special rope. The noise everyone made hurt my ears.

'Nan ate all her Rolos.

'Then the ringmaster said something ever so loudly. Would anyone from the audience like to try the trapeze? No one did, because it was far too scary and everyone was watching. Then Nan got up and said she would.'

Someone laughed, and Miss Atkins told them to shut up. 'Go on, Tom.'

'And they put my Nan in pink tights, and she went with them, and she was a bit scared, she told me later, but she didn't let it show. And she climbed up the ladder with the acrobats. Right to the very top. I think they stopped to let her get her breath back, but then they sat her on a swing and pushed it out over the crowd for her to get used to it. She looked really tiny all the way up there. Dad said she should come down, but I told him, no, it's OK, they know what they're doing. And they held my Nan and swung with her backwards and forwards, higher and higher, until the swing was nearly touching the roof. And one let Nan go, and she flew through the air and did a perfect somersault. She didn't fall. The other man, he caught her easily. She's only small.'

'Thank you, Tom,' said Miss Atkins. 'Who's next?'

And at break, Billy Brown said Tom was a liar, because where was the circus? And Sarah said he was a liar because no one's Nan could get to the top of a circus ladder, and no one wanted to play with him. And the break lady gave him an extra bun and said she was sorry.

When Tom got home after school, there was Mrs Pym Next Door in his house. She smelled of Vim. Dad was busy but he'd be back later.

Then he went to go upstairs, and got halfway up, trailing his hand on the wallpaper, when he remembered. The room seemed echoey without his small Nan in it, like the fireplace when the fire's gone out. There was no point in looking anywhere.

The only thing left of his Nan was her book on the bedside table, with a turned down page where she put it down last. Mrs Pym had made the bed, and it was cold and clean.

Sometime soon, not now because it wasn't right, he would pick up a pillow and bury his nose in it. He'd sniff so deeply, and through the clean smell of the pillowcase there would be some of his Nan's air left inside the pillow.

When he was ready.

Harry's Catch

HARRY GOES FISHING when he needs to be alone, needs to work things out, needs to say sorry. He needs to say sorry to his wife, Bren, but he doesn't know how. It's late afternoon and he's out in the old dinghy spinning for mackerel; first time he's felt like being alone since he had his scare, his pacemaker. Half a mile out and he's caught two. The fish are flapping in a green bucket with an old piece of plywood for a lid, in less than an inch of thin red water. It's odd, he thinks, how mackerel don't remember the difference between small fry and spinning hooks. Nothing's retained.

He's in the stern, right hand resting on the tiller, smoking. Knows he shouldn't. The outboard is idling, put-putting, and every so often the propeller lifts half-out of the water and the blades slosh and churn air. Landward, Harry sees his little Cornish village bobbing, the headland, the harbour, the beach, their shop, the grey church. The dunes and the caravan field. It's getting chilly. He zips his jacket, pulls the collar up.

There's a line over the side, fastened round the cross-strut of an old wooden 'H'. He pulls at it, holding the cigarette high between two fingers, feeling for weight. Now and again there might be the tug of a fish pulling back—then it's gone and Harry wonders if it was there at all.

Then, there's a tugging that comes straight up and finishes deep in his chest muscles.

He starts to wind the line in; turn by turn the fish gets heavier. Harry thinks about it breasting the sharp water, struggling. He thinks about it not winning, about it threshing into the air, about things unheard that will bubble from its throat. About droplets of water flying from its tail, blood on its scales.

Then he shakes his head, breathes deeply. Sea, engine oil, mackerel, blood, salt, tobacco. Lets his ears fill with the clatter of the old outboard, the slosh and clap of wavelets against the hull.

He took Bren out spinning for mackerel once, years ago. Just married and things settling, despite everything.

I've never liked fish, me, she'd said. *Not many fish in Bradford. Slimy, aren't they?* Then after laughing at catching one, she'd watched appalled, as Harry dehooked it and threw it, thrashing, into a box. *But it's dying. It's hurting. It's not right.*

She'd cried. Second time he'd seen that.

Now, Harry pulls on the line, playing the mackerel.

'Another catch. Big'un,' he says. But he's forgetting. He's alone.

～

Who is Harry? Just an ordinary bloke in his late fifties, getting away from the wife, having a think. Harry of Harry and Bren. Harry the newsagent. Harry the sweetshop, the grocer. Harry the shop-that-sells-everything-you-could-possibly-want-in-this-little-harbour-village. Harry with the license to sell alcoholic beverages. Who's up every morning at five thirty to sort the morning papers, take the milk delivery, semi and full, clotted cream in white plastic tubs, yellow curls of butter in cellophane. Chickens from the butcher's in St Merryn, delivered by the green van, with sausages in poly-trays, mince. Harry whose shop is closing soon.

Harry who had a health scare a month or so back. Suddenly couldn't breathe, one hand on the counter, one on the till. Bren gone to the wholesalers. Fifty nine years landing—thud—a fist on his chest, while a woman from the caravan site was talking to herself, *Cheddar or Double Gloucester? Why's the sell-by on the ham only tomorrow? Where's the Fairy Liquid?* and Harry's mouth hanging open with a trickle of spit running down his chin. He didn't want to move in case his heart might founder on his ribs having cut itself adrift.

The water is green here over the shoal. The line disappears, darker and darker green, filament straight. The fish is fighting and Harry was thinking then, as he pre-saw the fish hanging in the air, arcing, bucking, its eye fixed. Time. How it sheds like water dropping off fish scales and falls back into itself. How you can see into it, like deep water. How the further away it gets, backwards or forwards, the more impenetrable it is.

And of course, if it is covering dark things, like the shoal, it is darker still. Harry drags deep on his cigarette, holds it, his heart ticking in his ears like a death watch beetle.

Deep in the green he hears his father when they still had the farm, perched above him on the tractor, red faced. July, it was. Hot. Their five acre given over to the caravans for the first time and Harry, sixteen, helping out. *Don't want you mixing with their likes,* his father says, but then made him take the money. Help manoeuvre the vans. Drag a few out of the mud with the Ferguson. Deliver the milk, bread, remembering to add a few pence a time.

His flesh crawls now, giving up memories. The excitement of the 'Unknowns', new people in the village. People who stayed and played at house in flimsy caravans for five days, seven days, ten, fourteen. Unknowns with their kids and dogs, their other-place otherlife accents, blaring transistors, Brylcreemed hair. Their talk of factories. Social Clubs. Their smell. Aftershave and sweat. Their white shirts, rolled up sleeves, silver watches. Black trousers and side burns. And the girls. High breasted. Backcombed beehive hairdos and suspender belts when the village girls still had partings, kirbygrips, short socks and sandals. And their smell ... the beach. Cockles and mussels.

He rests his arm on the side of the boat, flips his cigarette into the water and watches the butt bobbing on the memories.

He hears himself in the caravan field, behind the communal wash house with its mud-spattered whitewashed walls and green scum under the outside tap, he and a girl called Janice, heady with beer and strange cigarettes. His voice, cracking, *Of course I've done it before,* and Janice, black roots and gold hair, her fast hand unzipping, playing him, his breathing hot, sharp, his fingers under, inside, slippery. He'd come over her fingers, her skirt. He hears the dripping of the scummy tap. The laughter. Then the lies to his mates on the harbour wall. *See her, that one, yellow skirt? I done it to her.*

Taking his mates up the hill to the caravan field later and calling for Janice, walking behind them all giggling down the lane, watching her thin ponyish calves, the blue-white of the backs of her knees when she hitched her skirt high over the stile, the flash of dark between her legs. To the dunes where she let them, one after the other ... in a pale hollow where a gull had made a meal of a catfish head and left bone, skin with a feeler still attached ... where he watched pale bums jumping in the marram. Where she said, *that's enough now, no more* and *please—no more*, then just *no, please,* but he hadn't done it yet. And where he did do it, slipped it in like a fish swimming against the current while two boys held her. *Uh, uh.* One two and he was gone.

He remembers fishing the next day, alone, marvelling at himself, Harry the man, standing different, shoulders straighter, legs braced against the rocking of his boat, every muscle in its place, taut and bragging. He remembers the mackerel that day, how he pulled the hooks from their mouths, tearing the skin because he could. How he squeezed their bodies, flapping, until their eyes bulged and their gills ran scarlet, dripping back into the sea, the gulls screaming.

Harry sighs. Checks the fish in the bucket, heaving and twitching against each other.

He'd lied to his parents over why he needed to see the doctor. He'd gone alone, sitting legs apart on the bus, jouncing through lanes alive with fuchsia and sunshine to be told he'd caught something with a name that belonged in text books, in jokes. In 'what not to do' books. In books that tell you you'll never get better from this. Learn to live with it. And one, found in the library, darkling on a dusty shelf, preaching that it was 'divine retribution for the profligacy of a generation'.

Time falling into itself, dark over its shoals.

Sixteen. That summer weighs heavy. Nothing was the same again. Even after they'd gone home the unknowns left themselves in the village like a virus. The local girls demanded hairspray from the shop. Spray deodorant. Pale lipsticks. The boys grew their hair and made cowlicks. Leaned against walls and smoked. Glowered, transistor radios to their ears.

Harry resumes winding the line. Watches the green water. Feels the fish thrashing, and between the movements, the steady pull of the lead weight. He wonders if it's true that, like they say, fish feel no pain, how on earth 'they' know, and if they use the right instruments to measure it. The weight making his arm, his shoulder, heavy, heavy.

Fair game, the girls in the caravans, every summer after that, on their factory social weeks. What was to lose? Jennys and Judys, Glorias and Gails. Stellas and Sheilas. Their black-horizoned eyes and stiff hair, their foreplay talk of machines and foremen, punch cards and union meetings. A different language. Different skin. White factory legs and tight skirts. Cockling and musselling in the marram and not a care.

Then Bren. Harry almost forgets to breathe. It's as though the little dinghy isn't big enough for the air he needs. Wonders if they'll invent a pacemaker for lungs. Wonders if pacemakers help the heart to love as well as beat when the heart throws in the towel? Not that he'd need that . . .

Bren, seventeen to his twenty three, with her high voice and small hands, the pulse in her neck like a moth caught under the skin. Bren who didn't smell of shellfish but ice-cream. Sweet. Her scalp. Sweet as new wood. That feeling that washed over him, prickling like sand blown across the beach. No marram. It was as though he was holding something made of glass, a bubble with freckles.

Harry does breathe in, deep, breathes in the mackerel smell, the blood, and shifts the plywood again with one foot. One fish is rigid. The other pulsates, its tail twitches; one eye locked on Harry, the other unseen, unseeing, touching the bottom of the bucket.

He's back there holding Bren's hand. That other summer. Sitting on the harbour wall, the swell of her little breasts rising, falling, like the sea. She talking about the city, chimneys, traffic, noise. Men called 'Sir'. Clattering typewriters. Ribbons that run out of ink. Changing jobs. Trams. Tickets. She saying that her name was really 'Bren the Clippie'. How it was so peaceful here, a sort of peace that settles right into your stomach. Harry hears her voice. Its edge. The way she said *me*, her lips in a smile, instead of *my*.

Peace, right here in me stomach, she said, patting her dress. Blue gingham. Harry knowing there's only two, three layers of cotton between her hand and her skin. Patting in time to the waves patting the side of Harry's boat as time drips off the scales and falls back into itself. Harry hears the sounds, sees the tiny hairs on her forearm in the sunshine, the lift of her chin and a white ear.

Eeeeeh, she says over the years, heels drumming on the granite blocks of the harbour wall, *but it's quiet, in't it?* as though she was in church and the quiet was too much. Two whole weeks of seeing her, between the farm work and the caravan field duties. 'Walking out' with someone infinitely precious like old couples did, and no funny business.

Until the night before Bren was due to go home. And that evening they walked on the headland away from the village, up past the pig farm, laughing at the smell, and on to where the rocks fell away into the sea like they'd been pushed and frozen. And there, the aloneness was too much, the sun going down was too much, the sound of the sea saying hushhh like a mother sending her baby to sleep was too much, and the high cry of a gull brought tears to Harry's eyes.

What's the matter? said Bren.

Harry, who thought it was the sound of the gull, found himself saying, *You. You're going home* and there, on the soft turf beside an outcrop of rock a little way off the path, Bren whispering over and over that she loved him, they loved each other, quietly.

Harry is sitting holding the line, a hot pebble rising in his throat, his eyes squeezed tight shut against the tears.

He thinks of a day not long after the loving, when the caravan field was empty, harvest almost over. A day when heat hung over the fields like a fire that would not go out and the air pressed in solid on all sides. Returning tired, hot, to the farm at the end of the day, leaving the tractor and trailer ready for the morning. His father waiting for him inside the front door. *You have a visitor.*

Going into the house, blinking in the sudden shadows. Brenda at the kitchen table fingering a best cup and saucer, tea untouched. Harry remembers, although he hasn't thought about this moment for years, that she was wearing a hat. A pale green sun hat pulled over one ear. Her eyes huge.

His mother taking him aside, out in the hall, hissing, *What is she here for?*

Sitting in the boat, everything is melting. The headland, the village, the harbour wall, solid granite melting and flowing, up, down. Harry remembers Brenda's words, slow, joyless, falling into the hot evening air like shovelfuls of dark earth on wood. *Who will want me now?*

And his reply.

It is the first time, here on the boat, that Harry has allowed himself to think in bright primary colours about his marriage to Bren. And the thinking spawns side-canals, full of deep green stagnant water, bubbles from the ooze staggering to the surface and breaking slowly.

No kids. Just in case. Now he looks at the dinghy, empty save him in the stern, and it's as though it weighs deeper in the water—carrying the ghosts of one, maybe two sons sitting there with him, fishing. Big now. Grown-up. The ghosts are joshing and play-punching, calling each other names, grinning. Calling Harry an old fart.

The line catches on something. Harry stands up and the boat rocks a little.

Steady on, old fart, say the ghosts.

Then one says, *Race you Dad,* and the voice is younger. Teenaged. Eager. Harry is walking to the pub, one son each side, and the door swings wide to let them all through laughing. *Get 'em in Dad.*

Then he hears, *take me fishing with you, Granpa?* and feels small hands pulling at his overall in the shop.

Harry shakes his head, blinks, and the boat is empty again. Silent. A herring gull is flying overhead, head down, eyeing the bucket.

Harry has freed the line. He gives it a tug. The fish is still there, pulling, and he is winding it in. There's a knot in the line. That's half way.

The farm sold, the shop bought. The agreement that there would be no other shop. The caravan field, smart, with its own laundry, the old wash house pulled down, a new shower block.

They were happy, weren't they, he and Bren?

Wasn't there happiness in choosing postcards by the hundred, betting which would sell out first? Always the cartoons. Making little shelves for the sweets, low down, for the kiddies to choose. Lugging the papers in their twine bundles. Doing the puzzles and crosswords on yesterday's before they were taken away. Wasn't there happiness in the deep scent of warm strawberries, raspberries in punnets from the villagers' gardens? Happiness in buying in that special Camp coffee for old Mr Brock, silver tweezers for Bella at the pub, oatcakes for Malcolm the harbourmaster.

Maybe less happiness in getting in goods for the caravan field. Multi-flavoured potato crisps. Chocolate spread. Sandwich spread. Bright orange drinks.

There was happiness in catching Brenda on the foldable steps, reaching up to put a bottle of gin on the top shelf, her blue overall rising round her thighs. Happiness in catching her tired at the end of the day, daydreaming, so far away she doesn't come back at first when he calls.

Earth to Bren? Where've you gone this time? His hand on her shoulder.

Nowhere love. Just woolgathering . . .

The fish is fighting hard now. Harry looks over the side, but can't see it yet.

Was there happiness in going to Church every Sunday? Harry looks back to the village, to the church squatting like a fat pigeon on its little hill above the houses. At least the church was always there, didn't change. Not like the caravan site—bought by a leisure company who replaced all the statics, planted little gardens, sold timeshares, made an area of wood-clad caravans like little log cabins, called the whole place 'Happy Lands'. Fifteen acres now. Most of what had been his father's farm. Rebuilt the washhouse. Added a whole row of shops. Surf gear. Launderette. Pizzas. General Stores.

Harry feels dizzy. Maybe too much sun this afternoon. He sees the caravan field, dotted with white like so many gulls on the waves. Checks the fish in the bucket again, and now they are both rigid, lying next to each other like blood-soaked lovers.

Sex. It was OK, wasn't it? They fell into a ritual, letting each other know by signals whether it would be on. Or whether the wanting would have to be enough. And always, even the times it was 'OK' there was a black beetle that spat tar waiting at the back of his mind, ready to bury its head beneath the skin and raise blisters that itched and wept. Harry even gave the beetle a name. Janice. Never really talked about it. It was just there, as immovable as the headland. As unpredictable as the sea.

Then. A few months ago, his heart. And he wonders if it may have worn out because he used it so much. But it's fine; he hardly knows he has a pacemaker, now. And Bren was marvellous. Everyone said.

But what does everyone know? Yesterday. Bren in tears in the kitchen, sitting at the table, straight backed, her hands round a blue mug, staring into it as though something would rise through the meniscus.

I don't love you, Harry, she said. *I can't find peace with you.*

Harry sighs, puts the wooden 'H' under his boot, lights another cigarette. He shuts his eyes, feels the lift and rock of the waves, and wonders whether the fish can feel waves under the surface. Whether surges happen on the sea bed and scramble families of mackerel, so that, if mackerel can love, they never find each other, ever again.

I have tried to love you, she said.

Harry pulls his collar up further. Smokes, taking in great lungfuls. The sky is grey, the sea is dark. Deep. His fish? He's forgotten the fish. He pulls on the line. It is still there on the end, he can still feel it struggling, but weaker now. The steady tug of the lead weight is more obvious. Closer to the surface. The last fifteen feet or so is thick green line, and he can see the fish now, a silver shape in a dirty greygreen sea.

I wanted to leave you, she said. *So many times.*

Bren looked at him in their kitchen and named them; the men she would have left him for. A litany of strong bodies, nearly thirty years in the telling. Villagers. Real fishermen. Farmers. An artist. A father of three who took a caravan five years running.

Did you sleep with any of them? Harry said through a haze, reaching for her hand, feeling her wrist bones. Seeing the moth struggling under the skin of her neck.

The mackerel breaks the surface. Writhes. Harry stands up, cigarette in mouth, swinging the fish high, watching it bucking, flicking silver and red droplets, hitting him, flailing at him, spattering his eyes, his lips.

Bren's voice was so quiet that Harry had to lean forward. *No Harry . . .* Her eyes, grey, looking straight at him yet through him, as though her gaze pierced his skull and fled, ending somewhere in a distant galaxy where there really was peace.

I loved them too much for that.

~

Harry sits down, gripping his fish behind the gills. He can feel the flesh moving under its scales. He could twist the hook out fast but he doesn't. The mouth gapes. Harry pulls the hook to the side. Keeps pulling. It stretches the mouth open, wider, wider, then slices through the cartilage, breaking it open. He

123

hears a high sound in his head and drops the spinning line on the floor of the boat. He is cold.

The mackerel drips blood onto his sleeve, its eye silver as a mirror. Harry leans forward, and, looking the fish in the eye, he presses the cigarette end to its flesh and holds it there, his hand shaking, until the hissing stops.

He kicks the plywood aside and throws the fish into the bucket where it lies across the others, flicking. He can see the burn on its side, dark. He reaches down and moves it, turns it over so that it is lying alongside the others, half in the water.

Harry leans back and listens to his heart in his ears. Like the rush of the tide coming in over the rocks. He keeps looking back at the fish, waiting for it to stop moving. Waiting for it all to be over. And when it is, when the fish does not move any more, he thinks that perhaps it is not quite dead, and nudges it. The fish shudders. Something slight pulling at a muscle.

∼

Harry lurches to his feet, staggers. He bends, picks up the bucket and throws it and its contents back into the sea with a shout, crimson-silver-green, and the herring gull that has been following the boat cries and swoops. Two dead mackerel torpedo rigid into the water but the new catch floats. The gull stretches its neck, its feet, its beak towards it, wings roiling the air, and Harry flicks his hand at the bird. But the bird persists, lunging at the fish and Harry waves his arms, shouts 'Get off you bugger!' and the bird hefts itself back into the air.

Harry leans out over the side, lowering his hand into the sea until the wavelets meet it and carry the mackerel into his palm. He cradles the fish loosely under the surface, letting the water flow over its body, lifting its gills. He moves his hand back and forth, back and forth, rocking the fish, willing it to have a heartbeat, his heartbeat, faster, panic, fear, pain; the embryo of a memory. His fingers relax. The mackerel lies there for a moment, flickers and is gone.

SIMON'S SKIN

THIS MORNING I put on Simon's skin. I was going to wear it for a day and a night. I was looking forward to being a bloke, even a bloke like Simon; I wanted to know what having a dick was like.

Simon's dick is kind of shrunken, like it wants to hide, like it's given up. Close by there are bruises, livid, deep, where he fishes around for a vein. Straight up. Faster that way. To the brain, no stops.

Simon's scalp is balding, buzz cut. He's grey at thirty-nine. I ran my fingers over his skull, felt the scars where he was hit with a half-brick in a street fight. They are ridged, like someone took a trowel to the head and planted something under the skin.

Simon's arms are thin. There are more bruises, old, faded, and if I hold his forearms up to the light, his skin's like thick translucent rice paper. It doesn't fit. It was made for someone stronger. I look underneath the top layer for the web of veins I know must be there. But these arms are alabaster. Pale. The hands are blue and swollen.

I inspect our legs. Somewhere under this skin is his skeleton, not mine. He's six foot, at least. Maybe that was part of the deal. Maybe this body-swap is total?

Simon's left leg below the knee is one big black brown purple ulcer. If I half close my eyes, it looks like a huge hole. The toes stick out of a bruised foot like ghosts.

126

SIMON'S SKIN

Simon's face peers out of the mirror at me, questioning. His eyes are full of apology. He is cowed, broken. I wonder if he's going to cry, but maybe not. Maybe there's just not the energy to make tears.

OK. I have a choice. I can carry on at skin level, playacting at being a man on Methadone, or I can really live it for a while. I can feel what he feels. That won't be just a bit of fun. I'll *feel* stuff; no preparation. No slide into it.

No matter. I know what having a dick is like and it's no big deal. Don't know what all the fuss is about. Of course; bring on the rest.

∼

Sickness. The deepest nausea I've ever felt floods up from my centre. It takes me over. Even my fingers ache with sickness. My mouth is filled with bile. I have to spit on the floor, once, twice, three times. I cup my hands, shaking, hold them under the cold tap, take a mouthful of water which burns as it goes down.

I'm bending at the sink and my knees protest. Every movement I make, my ankles, toes, knees, hips, every vertebra, my neck, shoulders, elbows and wrists, every finger joint, they scream. Ground glass has been eased under the skin and the bones rub together jarring and setting off sparks.

My head is full of wire wool. Or sand bags. It is so heavy. I want to lay it down somewhere, take it off, anything. My eyes are lead, and hot, they might melt and run down my face. My eyelids are edged with barbed wire.

∼

127

I am standing in the bathroom trying to wash Simon's skin. Making it feel a little better so when he wears it again it will have healed a little. I run the shower and step inside.

It's too cold, then too hot. The water is razor blades then pellets of fire. The soap stings under my arms, between my legs, in all our folds and dark places. I wash his hair. That feels good, at least, rubbing the half-brick scar, smoothing it. Running my fingers along his eyebrows as though he were a child trying to sleep and I am helping him to go.

I lean against the tiles, close my eyes, and listen to the water howling down the drain.

I hold my dick, and I ache.

I'm thinking. Maybe I won't give this skin back.

I pat him dry with a yellow towel, and use baby powder. I splash his face with cool water and use a cream which sinks into his skin like he's been dying in a hot, dry desert for a hundred years. I make him drink five glasses of water. Two come up again, but that's OK.

I walk to my bed and lie him down. I pull the duvet up over our legs, and the ulcer screams with the weight. I turn on his side and draw the duvet up to his chin. His chin grazes my knuckles. I guess I should have shaved, but I wouldn't know how.

Then I lean across and switch off the light, hugging myself, himself, like I was hugging him to sleep. Sleep is a great healer, they say.

Maybe when I wake, I'll think about this. Maybe I'll find my own skin, wherever I left it, put it on again. But now, drifting off, it seems a far better thing to stay Simon.

CLOSED DOORS

THINK ABOUT IT. If what you do is clean shoes, you have no need to talk. If, like Matt, you are seventeen, and what you do is collect, wipe, brush and buff shoes left at night outside bedroom doors on the sixth floor of the Grand Hotel, Eighth Avenue, you have no need to talk. What is there to talk about when you are dealing with other people's shoes?

He does not talk but he makes ghosts as he cleans the shoes, as he buffs them, as he polishes them, well after midnight night after night. He conjures wavering shapes in his head; shapes that rise out of those black lace-ups with their heels neatly against the wall, or those scuffed blue slip-ons left together just outside a door. There are always clues, cues for the ghosts.

Then, the ghosts float in the windowless corridor, peopling it, sliding past the small cupboard next to the lift where Matt sits on the floor, working. Some sit next to him and whisper as he works. He tries to keep them in his head, take them home with him, back to the hostel on Fifty Third where old men drink and young men still dream.

ROOM 601: *Man's tan brogues, badly scuffed, size eleven. Red patent leather high heeled shoes, hardly worn, size five.*

Matt rubs a red shoe with a cloth, closes his eyes. Slowly, like the last wisps of smoke rising from a dying bonfire, a young

129

woman takes shape, small featured, apologetic. She has a withered left arm. He sees her tucking long brown hair behind her ears, straightening a denim jacket, trying out a smile, then climbing narrow stairs, carrying a small violin case in her good hand. He sees her straightening her shoulders, looking bright. She holds her withered arm close to her body; she flexes the fingers, bent like twigs on a branch.

She opens the violin case and takes out a child's violin. She walks to a window, lifts the violin to her chin and begins to play, smiling over the music.

The brogues are old, dusty. The heels are worn at the sides, left shoe more than right. The shoes are scuffed along their inner edges, as though they rubbed together. This is the man who found a child's violin for the woman, taught her to play. He is older, worn down like his shoes. He limps.

The room where he teaches is filled with sun, with books, with music scores, fossils, shells, sea urchins. He has left the door to his bedroom ajar; the young woman glances at an unmade narrow bed, and she turns away, lowers her head, plays on as the sun throws a halo round her. For a second the man forgets to breathe, and when he does, when he opens his chest and breathes in deeply, he feels dizzy.

ROOM 603: *Man's dark brown lace-ups. Size nine. Woman's brown slip-ons, low heeled, size four.*

Matt sees a lonely grey-suited man with an empty navy suitcase and matching overnight bag, computer case, toupee. He sees the man brushing the toupee, placing it on a side table next to a bottle of whiskey. His living room has chairs, settees pushed back against the walls like a waiting room. No flowers,

130

no photos, no books. He pours a whiskey, takes off his shoes and sits down to read a newspaper. He cannot settle. Sighs, checks a number, and makes a call.

'How is my mother today? Is she well? No pain? Will you brush your fingers across her forehead when she sleeps, let her think someone is kissing her goodnight? Thank you. Next month? I will call by next month, if . . .'

Matt sees him packing the suitcase, folding shirts, handkerchiefs, underwear. He sees him packing an old Bible, and a pair of old women's brown slip-ons, low-heeled. He sees him placing those shoes alongside his own outside foreign bedroom doors.

ROOM 605: *Man's black lace-ups, old, dusty, size ten. Woman's black court shoes, dusty, badly scuffed heels, size six.*

Matt runs his fingers over the man's shoes, tracing a small snake in the dust, and he thinks of graveyards, neat grass, regiments of white stone, endless paths of gravel. He sees a man, still strong but fading, his hand on a white stone, and Matt feels the man stroking the stone as he might a woman, a baby, unthinking and transported. The man raises reddened eyes to the horizon, where the stones merge into a solid white line, stone on stone as far as he can see.

The woman puts her hand on his shoulder, murmurs something about always being together. They turn and walk slowly after the mourners, all of them black and silent, towards a line of black cars like low beetles on the grass. The man and the woman walk past the cars.

Matt sees the couple in a coffee house, relaxed, steam rising from cappuccinos, smiling, quietly dipping almond biscuits. A newspaper neatly folded on the table beside them, open at the funeral announcements; four today, a few tomorrow neatly ringed in blue pen.

ROOM 607 *Man's deck shoes, brown, size eleven. Woman's flatties, green leather, size six.*

A couple who no longer speak. He a cuckold, she a fishwife, they do not speak save through their dog, a spaniel.

'Tell my wife I am hungry.'

'Tell him he'll have to wait.'

They live in the same house, eat at the same table, listen to the same music, read the same books, sleep in the same bed, but they never speak save through the dog.

'Tell her I got promoted today.'

'Tell him I am happy for him.'

The dog, with golden ears and weeping eyes, sleeps in their bedroom.

'Tell her I haven't forgotten our Wedding Anniversary. I have arranged a night away.'

'Tell him I am happy.'

Matt feels the silence, for the Grand Hotel does not accept dogs. The couple can make silent love; after all, it is away from their battlefield.

ROOM 609: *Woman's cream court shoes, brown trim, size five and a half.*

Her apartment is full of flowers, mirrors, silver photograph frames, white porcelain horses. A granite and smoked glass table, white grand piano, palm trees in pewter pots. She is tall, statuesque, chic grey hair and short nails.

132

Interesting intelligent men, men from agencies, nice men, screened men, accompany her to theatres, operas, dinner. Afterwards, they wait discreetly for her to want sex. She does not.

She travels, discovers, appraises, marvels. She attends auctions, buys art for the Metropolitan. Degas, Monet, Manet. An unknown Whistler from Paris, a Turner watercolour from Florence.

In her suitcase, always, wherever she goes, there is a lacquer box; a box with a label in childish writing, 'The most beautiful things in the world'. The box contains amethyst crystals hidden in the heart of a broken grey stone, a photograph of an old woman in a wheelchair, a letter from a murderer on Death Row, and a desiccated eight week foetus curled in cotton wool.

ROOM 611: *Man's patent leather slip-on, grey, size eight and a half. Right foot only.*

The patent leather feels smooth, cool, expensive. A narrow foot, fine-boned and light like a bird. A dark study, no windows, three walls lined with bookshelves, floor to ceiling, papers piled on floorboards, more books, maps, files, spectacle cases. On the fourth wall, shelves of single shoes, one a year since 1941, size eight and a half, right foot only.

This man, a Jew with the skeleton of a bird, hunched, always asks for room number 11, no matter which floor. He visits once a year, the same date, visits the synagogue, stays, head bowed, lost in thought. He visits the University, stands in front of the young, and talks of his time in a Silesian camp. He cannot say the name.

He talks gently, his voice cracked with age like an old bell, and the students supply him with a microphone which he does not use. Instead he drops his voice, and the students lean forward to hear him, drawn into his space.

He does not talk specifically about Block 11, about a week without food, about drinking his own water until there was none, about licking salt sweat from the bodies of the dying. About eating his own shoes to live.

Adonai, he'elayti min shaol . . .

The man with the skeleton of a bird who will fly soon, washes carefully. Naked, he sits on a white towel, takes a sharp knife, cuts into smooth grey leather, and prays as he chews.

$\sim$

It is four in the morning. Matt lies awake at the hostel, listening to old men snoring, a helicopter clattering overhead looking for lost souls. He cleaned his quota of shoes at the hotel, replaced them all, and as he left down the back stairs, he might have heard a violin playing.

Tasting Pebbles

MY SISTER, MAY. She woke to the spectrum of birdsong on light mornings. A thousand mother-of-pearl flakes of confetti showering her bed. Sugar on her tongue. I can hear her voice: *they are my colours, listen.*

I am no poet, but she might have been. The one who said: *this is how it is* and I let the words run through my fingers like sand. Like water. Now, I try to remember, and it is like drawing that water from a dark well.

Water, she said, was dark blue knives, sharp as flint, the sound; the feel of it slippery elongated esses. The scrape of knife on toast was green gloss of holly leaves, avalanches on distant mountains, and the taste of butter round and grey like a polished pebble.

On the beach I stared at pebbles. Held them in my hands, brought them to my lips. Ran my tongue over them quietly. To me, they were just pebbles, and I would be told to put them down.

Even voices, for May, were not only sounds. She said when our mother spoke it was green hills rising and falling, bitter Christmas chocolate; our father's voice the rainbow of petrol on water, the sharp wrinkle of dried orange peel. I closed my eyes to listen, but to me they spoke only words.

The well gives up images, slowly. A laughing May, running, filling her lungs not with air, but sparks. May pressing her cheek against the wall of our house, saying *it hums like bees, listen!* Running her fingers up and down, eyes shut, smiling, *try it. I feel them, soft as mud.*

I remember her staring at my school book, grimacing, hands over her ears to shut out the clamour. She said print was noisier than pictures. I laughed. It was my turn to see things that she didn't. I could read.

I can hear our teacher, a nice woman who came to our house. *Today we are doing A for Apple. Let's all colour an A red like an apple,* as she must have said it to a generation, but never anyone like my sister. May asked how she could colour her A when it was making the sound of drums. She said *what colour is the sound of a drum? It's like leather shoes.* The nice woman handed her a red crayon, and asked me to come and help.

I helped. I helped my sister to shut her mind, and she lost her colours. May earned the label 'slow', and I was the one going for other colours, other trophies. I understand it now, what it must have been like for her. Without her colours to guide her, where were the signs? They no longer moved round her tongue like clever ants leaving drops of nectar where she least expected it. Without shapes and textures, moving bricks like mud, where was the joy of touch? Without flights of motes in the air when she looked skywards, what was the point of looking up?

Why do we choose what we do, making our way through life? For me, choices were ruled by my need to keep ahead of May. Teaching, joining the nice women who close young minds? Perhaps. May, I see now, wept for her colours; she looked for them everywhere. She worked in a pottery, where she fed cold wet slip to thin fingers. A florists, where she was surrounded by green smells and clashing colours. For a while she breathed in sweetness and warmth in a kitchen making biscuits, kneading small shapes that would flatten and melt on the tongue.

She told me how she felt with her first man, and I think it almost opened up again. The first time for May, letting go completely, sparks flying under the fingers of a man who chose her, she was breathless, she said, with the rushing in her ears, the soft fire of skin on skin in skin, the melting, warm velvet pulsing, and freshness of colour afterwards as though it had rained behind her eyes.

I ached. It was not like this for me.

Tell me, I said, turning my head away. What had she touched? A crush of colours, tangled threads of taste, salt and honey, artichoke and bitters, ripe plums, juice dripping off her chin, the smell of balsam. What had she felt? Smoothness, a raw white slip of the tide, rushing over flat sand, lace edged. What had she heard? The sea, she said, the tide rising and pulling, leaving the sand rippled and furrowed, bringing her almost to the point of having it all, then dropping her like so much froth, gasping like a fish.

He never knew about her colours. He knew about uniforms, about the sadness of leaving May alone for months, about leaving her waiting for letters. The sounds he knew split the ear sending him reeling over the sand. He can't have known the night held anything other than green images behind a mask; the whine of missiles.

Then, after he could not return, she spent her nights crying into the pillow, his khaki jacket bundled at her side. I was there and I heard her. She burned for the body not at her side, the body that was beneath other sand now, unmoving.

I was with her when their baby came. When she wept for the agony of it, bruising, raw, tearing and bloody. When she lay, deflated, it was me seeing the ceiling as a mass of blue light, and her body a hush of deep blood rolling over the sheets. I cried when the swing doors clashed as they ran with her child. When they came at May with masks and needles it was me lying with her, holding her, her body rigid. She could not weep.

When she stood in the window, barefoot on the tiles, her toes curling in the chill, whiteness under her feet, looking unseeing at a square of paper holding small foot and hand prints, I was there. She said then that somewhere behind her head there was a shimmer of petrol on water, green hills, bitter chocolate, dry oranges.

She had no escape, and I could not help her. It was as though she was in a roofless tower, she said, made of hard stone, a tower so high that she could not feel the air. Now, I understood. It did not take much for her to accept another body, who wept for his lost friend in May's bed. It did not take much to touch May. I know, that for a while, beneath his tears, rising to him, she felt the tide, felt the cliffs and the pound of waves on rock, the distilling of her grief into a million drops of spray against a leaden sky.

A small step then to other bodies, her hands feeling for the ripples on the sand. I think she felt grey walls closing over her head after monochrome coupling. Some, one or two, were kind, and then, briefly, the walls melted like spun sugar.

Is this how it was, for her? How it might have been for me? Maybe, when they played her, she heard the sea. Maybe, caught in a net, she rolled in the waves and smiled. Maybe, thrown up on the sand, she gasped like a fish, and waited. I can't ask her now, but I have to believe she heard the glitter of mother-of-pearl confetti piling round her bed. She felt the pulse of skin on skin, the taste of honey and iron on her tongue. The well of blood under her fingers trailing along flint walls.

She was just waiting for the tide to turn.

FUCK MAGNOLIA

I CLIMBED THE chain link fence by the railway today, Emmie. Sat down against the old brick wall and cried. It's weird, the closer you get to the graffiti the less you see. There's fresh stuff now. Tags, over and over, black and yellow. The rest? It's there, underneath.

Someone's valuing the house tomorrow. You know what's the worst bit? Painting over our walls, our words, before he comes.
 It's still there, my scrawled letters all round the sitting room,

WE COME FROM NOTHING,
WE GO TO NOTHING.

OH, COME ON
WHITBY AIN'T THAT BAD.

The F wobbles. There's a red drip. That's where you called downstairs, 'Mikey? Can you help?' I didn't fucking come up. Thought it was a light bulb gone, a spider . . . Jesus.
 You'd gone up for a bath . . . said, 'Join me?'
 The day before, you found out they were building flats between us and the railway. You wouldn't see the brick wall, the tags, the scribble, the slogans. Your Modern Art. You said, 'Who does this graffiti, Mike? Why? You never see them, is it kids?'

You loved it, but it made you sad. So I wanted to do some, make you laugh.

When we met, you said your graphic design, my painting and decorating were the same thing. I thought Oh yeah dead samey. But you were right, we just came at it from different angles. You saw shapes, letters, everywhere. I remember we had some silly argument once. You were so stiff, standing like a little tin soldier, back rigid. I held your shoulders, bent, kissed you to shut you up. You laughed, said, 'When you kissed me we made a 'D'.' I didn't understand. You rearranged us, said, 'Now, look down at us.'

I only see colours, textures. I know about ragging, rolling, graining, scumbling, stencilling. No one wants it round here. I get excited when a call comes, 'Mike? Could you do a three-bedroom Victorian terraced?' I go, see colours to take it back to its roots, dark sensuous stuff, shining mahogany banisters, deep cream paintwork. Gaslight colours. Then, 'We've chosen plain Magnolia.'

That graffiti in the sitting room, Emmie. Fuck Magnolia! I wanted to paint something quickly, so when you came down from your bath, you'd see, you'd be pink and white, your hair in damp curls on your neck, you'd smell of powder, you'd be soft, in your slippers. Your head would come up to somewhere near my heart and this bloke would melt.

You made me laugh. You made me . . . No, you MADE me. That's it. After you, there's nothing much, Ems. How can someone so small leave such a gaping hole?

I cry. People try to snap me out, try to move me on like some animal that's down on its haunches waiting to die. I can't move. I don't know what to do without you.

You shouted down again, in a bit. I was balancing on the arm of the settee, painting letters fast: *Whitby ain't that bad* like a crazy man, thinking, She'll have my guts for garters.
    'What?' I yelled.
    Is heaven like Whitby? Every shade of white, isn't it? I bet there's no graffiti up there.

TODAY IS THE FIRST DAY OF THE REST OF YOUR LIFE . . .

    It's still scrawled over the bathroom mirror. It makes me think. Yesterday, I nearly . . . but I didn't. The day before that I nearly . . . but I didn't. They say when the scent of someone goes then they go too. I still wake up smelling you next to me, Emmie. Before I open my eyes you're there. Then I open them quick, to trick you into BEING there.

I found the appointment card yesterday. Doctor something— Doctor Shit. I wanted to punch the bastard. He walked his fingers over you like you were meat. I thought, OK, one millimetre closer and I'll stop those fingers Chum. I thought of me, then, your back arching, my mouth where his fingers were.

Hey lady, I miss you. I miss us. I miss it.

You said, 'Remember that wall, Mikey?'
    You'd been told you needed more tests and you wanted me to think about the wall?

You laughed. 'It says HUMANS ARE INEDIBLE. THEY CON-
TAIN TOO MUCH DDT.'

You asked if you would be inedible afterwards.

'Fuck me, Mikey.' You never said things like that. You'd
shrunk. You were glass in the bed Emmie, I didn't want to
break you. I couldn't. It didn't feel right, you whimpering, needing. You didn't come, I didn't.

In the night I woke and you were at the window.

I do this now. I squeeze my eyes shut, you are at the window.
I see the curve of your back, your arms, crossed, your head on
one side. You're naked, leaning against the window frame,
watching for the trains. The flats are too high to see the wall
properly. There's a streetlight. It picks out your cheek, shines
through your hair like candyfloss, like the spray from a spray
gun. I want to get up, come to you, hold you, make it OK.

Remember the poster when we went to the hospital? Some pic
of a newborn baby?

THE FIRST THREE MINUTES OF LIFE ARE THE MOST DAN-
GEROUS, it said, and when we'd checked you in (like a flaming
dirty weekend) you asked for a marker pen, we had to find the
poster again: you wrote THE LAST THREE ARE PRETTY CHAL-
LENGING AND ALL.

You were so bloody brave. Never said anything. Held my
hand like it was me hurting, they gave you the pre-med and
you said, 'Lie down with me?'

Like it would be difficult? You were so warm I nearly went to
sleep.

I can't remember what I did while you were away. They
brought a bed, one wheel didn't work, it stuck, it squeaked. You

143

came back. I wanted to get back into bed with you, I wanted you to wake up with me.

They said no.

Christ, Emmie, it was like looking at someone else, you smelled different. Suddenly you were ill.

I didn't want you to wake up. Not like that. You had gone, gone to sleep.

I thought (I'm so sorry. . . .) It's easier if she goes now. Forgive that, Ems?

It was funny when you came home. You walked in like this place was strange. Like it was a joke, the last few years. You were tired. Went upstairs, didn't come down. I came up with a cuppa, you were in the window again. The flats had grown, you said, like someone was pushing them up through the ground. They'd stuck scaffolding up, a metal web. Like a robot spider, you said. You couldn't even see the edge of the wall.

Where do I go from here? I'm not even thirty, and I'm lost, Emmie. Whatever there is, it's half, a quarter, an eighth, a six-teenth of what it would have been . . . and I wonder . . . it's like,

I AM SCHIZOPHRENIC.
I NEED SOMEONE TO TALK TO.
WHERE AM I WHEN I NEED ME?

I feel half of me is gone.

Blank cream flats in front of our house. You missed the trains in the night. You could still hear them, you said, because sound bounced, curved over the flats, and it would do that when they were finished.

It does.

'Six weeks,' they said. You were quiet for a bit and I didn't know what to say except I wanted to scream, shatter the walls, stop this. 'I love you, Emmie...' You walked over to the hospital window as though you'd see the railway, like there was your wall out there, and you said, 'Mike? When they say I've got six weeks, what do they mean? Do they mean it might be longer? Or less? Or tomorrow? They might be wrong, mightn't they? They might have things mixed up with some woman from another bed? It's just... I haven't finished yet. I have no children to carry my face.'

How did I answer that?

I was still working then. Went to this house a few days later to do a kitchen-diner. Yellow, white for a change. Nice woman, made me a coffee. There were two photos stuck behind some beading, her kids, two lads where she'd see them when she was cooking.

'How's things?' she said. 'Busy?'

The tap was running. I had the paint pot in one hand. *Canary.*

'My wife's dying.' I said.

I stopped working after that.

Coupla weeks in, you asked to walk down to the railway. We did, arms round like we'd just met. We'd never been this close to the old wall. Couldn't get over the chainlink ... but the bricks were old, crumbling. Words painted over, over, over, 'Like generations' you said. Then you saw

CITY ARE WANCERS

145

You leaned into me, looked up, giggled, 'What are wancers?'

My throat closed up. I remember thinking then, some fucker is going to paint out my Emmie like she's never existed.

We walked back past the building site, you stopped for a breather, held on to some scaffolding. Your ring tapped the metal, sound rang along the pole like an organ pipe. You tapped again, rested your head against the scaffolding, listening. 'Hey, it's Tubular Bells, that Mike Oldfield . . .' The sound belled around us, the whole structure rang.

Must have been one of the last times you went out, hey? Remember that nurse, the fat one, she clicked her tongue as she worked, never looked neat, nothing stayed tucked in? There was routine, it lulled. I thought this would be how it was now. You in bed, me telling you how the building was going.

No chance.

'We need to give her something stronger today.'

'That's fine, that's good, isn't it? She won't feel anything?'

'She'll float a bit.'

'Oh, right.'

'Mike? You may want to speak to her before . . .'

And I did.

I asked her to stay, the fat nurse. No, silly girl, not like that . . . so we could sleep, you and me, so you'd be OK. I needed to get out a couple of times. For air.

Ems, you always said Sundays were quieter days, even when they are noisy they are quieter than the rest. Like something's waiting to happen. Early in the morning anywhere is covered in a hush. Even the trains are quieter.

FUCK MAGNOLIA

I woke with you that Sunday, twined round you. I was in my jeans, jumper, hadn't wanted to move, slept, the only sound I could hear when I woke was the squeak of your syringe driver, chemicals floating you out. I didn't want to let you go. I thought I could keep you warm . . .
  It was ages, then I slid out of bed, called the nurse.
  I said, 'She's gone.'
  She held your wrist. Felt your neck. 'No, not yet.'
  That's when I said, 'Stay with her?'
  It was early, maybe five thirty. So quiet.
  Then our street was filled with sound, Emmie. Did you hear? Metal on metal. Up on the scaffolding round the new flats, a couple of storeys up, close as I could get to opposite our window. I hit the metal with a spanner, first it was tentative, apologetic, then I couldn't see, Ems. I hit out louder, louder, LOUDER, clanging, banging . . . LOUDER, Emmie, regular, each blow ringing along the pipes, fucking Tubular Bells, Ems, I just wanted to see you at the window, standing there smiling, telling me to stop . . .
  I hoped you'd know what I'd done. Maybe you felt it, heard it? They say hearing is the last to go. But you'll never be gone totally, not really. Look Ems, it's still there, on the clean cream walls of the flats, huge red letters, shouting it over and over, like the bell chimes . . .

EMMA WAS HERE

EMMA WAS HERE

EMMA WAS HERE

ACKNOWLEDGEMENTS

'I Can Squash The King, Tommo' was first published in *The 2007 Bridport Prize Anthology* having been awarded Second Prize by Tracy Chevalier. 'Words from a Glass Bubble' appeared in *The 2007 Fish Prize-Winner's Anthology* having won Second Prize, judged by Michael Collins, Dame Fiona Kidman and Clem Cairns. It was also runner up in Willesden Herald 2007, judged by Zadie Smith. 'Dodie's Gift' won the 2006 Willesden Herald Short Story Competition, again judged by Zadie Smith and was published in *Cadenza Magazine* where it also won a first prize, as 'Yellow Diggers, Dead Crows, Gifts'. 'The Lych Warmer was long-listed in the 2006 Bridport Prize. 'Cactus Man' was published by Honno Welsh Women's Press in their 2007 anthology *Safe World Gone*. 'There Were Tigers' won a prize in the inaugural Momaya Competition and was published in *Momaya Review*. 'The Carob Tree' won Cotswold Writers Competition, 'Fuck Magolia' (as 'Graffiti') was published in *Bravado Magazine* (New Zealand). 'Kettle on the Boat' won an award at London Writers' Inc, 'Closed Doors' was commended at *Winchester Writers' Conference*, 'Irrigation' won The Seventh Quark Phoenix Prize and was published in *Riptide Journal*. 'Harry's Catch' first appeared in *Night Train*, 'Smoking, Down There' in *Eclectica*, 'On the Edge' in *BuzzWords*, 'Bones' in *Smokelong Quarterly*, 'Excavation' in *Ascent Aspirations*, 'Simon's Skin' in *The Angry Poet* and a much shortened version was also runner-up in the Fish One-Page competition 2006, 'Tasting Pebbles' was published in *Thema* (USA) and *The Quiet Feather* (UK).

To the judges and editors of the above. Thank you.

Thanks also to Fish Publishing, Bantry, Ireland, home of the Fish Short Story Prize, for their generosity and for releasing my work early. To Maggie Gee and Jacob Ross for their kindness, inspiration and for their generous endorsements. To Peter James for his. To so many writers and friends who have been supportive along the way, especially Sue Booth-Forbes of Anam Cara Writers' and Artists' Retreat, Zoe King, Kay Sexton, my Brighton writing group, all at The Fiction Workhouse, The Dinner Ladies who are (amazingly) still my friends and The VIPs.

Love and thanks to my dear parents, to my husband Chris, our sons Nick and Toby and my daughter in law Nats. They all tolerate this strange person I have become since falling in love with writing.

Almost finally, a writer who showed me that the lightest touch leaves the deepest impression: Alex Keegan. Finally: Jen Hamilton-Emery and Salt Publishing. A quality lot and fun with it.

Really finally: to all those writers who I will never meet, but whose words are my teachers. Especially W G Sebald, Raymond Carver, Italo Calvino and John Cheever.

Lightning Source UK Ltd.
Milton Keynes UK
09 October 2010

160965UK00001B/22/P